CRITTERS

Brown Ghost Hunting Dog vol 3
Ghostly Stories of Furry Friends

Collection Edited By
J. A. Campbell

Inkwolf Press

Ghost Hunting Critters
Brown, Ghost Hunting Dog
Volume 3

All Rights Reserved
Ghost Hunting Critters Compilation Copyright © 2017 by
J.A. Campbell
Cover Design © 2017 by Shoshanah Holl

First Inkwolf Press Publication / August 2017

Gasper the Ghost Hunting Goldfish © 2017 Sam Knight
Brown and the Allosaurus Wrecks © 2017 Julie Campbell
Kotori and the Demons © 2017 Laura Hargis
Harbinger © 2017 Carol Hightshoe
Ferry Horse © 2017 Denise Harrison
Kitty and Pitty © 2017 Shoshanah Holl
Guardian © 2017 Rebecca McFarland Kyle
Petri and the Spirit Walker © 2017 Jessica Brawner
Clyde and the Ghost Cat © 2017 Jamie Ferguson
Taker of Young © 2017 Dana Bell
Morior Invictus © 2017 Alison Baumgartner
First Dog © 2017 Julie Campbell
Kills Like River © 2017 Jon Zenor

ISBN-13: 978-1974512904
ISBN-10: 1974512908

Published by Inkwolf Press
P.O. Box 251
Severance, Colorado
80546-0251

www.inkwolfpress.com
www.writerjacampbell.com

PRODUCED IN THE UNITED STATES OF AMERICA

10 9 8 7 6 5 4 3 2 1

Dedication

To all the special animals in our lives, past, present, and future, and to the veterinarians who lovingly care for them.

Editor's Note and Acknowledgements

This project started, as many of my projects do, by a conversation with Shoshanah Holl. She was telling me about a story idea she had for my world, and I told her she should write it. It didn't take long for that conversation to evolve into an entire anthology with a handful of authors who also wanted to play in my Ghost Hunting Dog world. The results, you hold in your hand.

I couldn't be more pleased with the quality of stories everyone turned in. They are fantastic. Some contain nods to the world I created, some use Brown as a character, and some simply take place in a world that could quite easily be the same as Brown's world. They're all fantastic.

When I first read all the stories, I worried about how I would arrange them, but after some excellent advice from Sam Knight (tell a story with the entire collection) it all fell into place. You'll see that the stories are arranged in groups and start in Brown's time. They move from there into our present, and the future, before making their way into the distant past.

At the end of the anthology you'll find a few true accounts of ghostly interactions by some of our authors.

I want to thank all of my contributors, not only for the quality of work they submitted, but for taking the time and having the enthusiasm to play in the Ghost

Hunting Dog world. I'm honored you all were willing to contribute to this collection. Thank you.

And thank you, dearest reader, because without your continued support these collections would remain unwritten, unshared, and that would be a sad thing indeed.

Table of Contents

GASPER THE GHOST HUNTING GOLDFISH

BY SAM KNIGHT

New Mexico, 1902

The rumble vibrating through the water in my bowl soothed me and I dreamed of when I lived in open water, subject to the random currents caused by wind and temperature changes. I thought it was thunderstorms off in the distance. We'd had a lot lately and last night was one of the worst ever.

Johnathon, my human, hadn't yet opened the fancy lace curtains veiling our picture window to Main Street, so I continued to doze, slowly fluttering my fins, enjoying the lazy morning. All of the humans went to church Sunday mornings, including Johnathon, so Sundays were our little pawnshop's quietest mornings. We were closed for business, out of respect, Johnathon told me, but we often hosted the Sunday Luncheons. Everyone loved to look at

Johnathon's collection of mysterious trinkets. And to come see me.

Shadows moving rapidly back and forth across the curtains roused me from my dream. The humans in our little town didn't usually hurry around so quickly. I heard shouting, which surprised me. I didn't often hear the sounds humans made outside of the immediate room my bowl was in. Walls tended to muffle all but the deepest and loudest noises.

Like the growing rumble.

As the shadows raced by, I found myself swimming in nervous circles. I don't usually feel restricted by my inability to swim through the air, and I haven't often regretted my decision to live above the surface with Johnathon, but as more humans shouted and ran by, I began to feel trapped in my bowl.

The alarm bell at the General Store clanged and I knew something was wrong. Since the new church bell arrived, the old iron one was only used in emergencies.

I tried to relieve my anxiety by swimming quickly. I hurried back and forth in a straight line, instead of my usual circles, so I could keep an eye facing the window each time I turned. I knew Johnathon would come for me soon.

The alarm bell stopped, but the strange rumbling noise had grown disconcertingly loud, and the humans' shouting, though still desperate and fevered, began to fade. They were moving away. I panicked.

My circles increased in speed, agitating the water until I accidentally slopped some over the side of the bowl and nearly rode my own wave out onto the parlor's expensive Persian carpet.

Startled, I stilled myself and stared down at the mess, hoping the water wouldn't stain the carpet.

I wasn't worried Johnathon would be upset with me, but he was very proud of the fancy carpet and had worked hard to get it all the way out here. I still couldn't quite fathom the idea it had come from across a salty lake bigger than the sky, but I had no reason to think Johnathon would fib to me. He was a very good and honest human. After all, he had changed my water nearly every day for fifteen years now.

Still, the careless splash bothered me. Fighting off nerves, I swam up and gulped air straight from above the surface to clear my head.

The odd vibration now shook my bowl enough that ripples formed and crashed around the edges. It reminded me of a buffalo herd thundering past our wagon when Johnathon and I traveled out from the East, and I wondered if that was what could be causing the vibration.

That would explain the upset humans, I thought, as I eyed the darker coloration on the carpet where my splashed water had landed.

Clattering sounds caught my attention. Vases, boxes, and curios on the shelves rattled and shook. The tintype photograph of a young Johnathon and his father standing next to a fossil dig fell from the wall. The fossil from the photograph, giant round jaws so large they reached over halfway to the floor, bounced against the wall, looking like they were trying to snap at me.

I hated looking at those giant, ragged teeth. They already gave me nightmares, and seeing them move like this was positively unnerving.

Suddenly my bowl lurched forward, sloshing out more water and sending me swimming desperately downward, trying to stay inside. My little pocket of water in this world of air slid to the edge of the table and threatened to follow the spill down to the floor. My bowl teetered on the edge, forcing me swim away from the edge as hard as I could.

I didn't really think I could stop the fall, but I tried anyway.

My bowl *thunked* back into place and stabilized, water sloshing back and forth violently, bobbing me up and down against my will. As the turbulence slowed, I bellowed my gills, looking down at the now much larger dark spot on the rug. Imagining myself lying there, I was torn between swimming up for another gulp of straight air or trying to bury myself in the rocks at the bottom and hiding.

Movement pulled my attention away from morbid thoughts. Someone tried to open the front door. No—something was coming under the door!

Muddy water foamed through threshold and every crack in the building lower than half the height of a human began spouting silty water. The muck, oozing in, rapidly spread out and engulfed Johnathon's beautiful carpet. In seconds, our little shop was flooded.

"Gasper!"

Johnathon! His voice carried in from the outside. I swam to the top and used my mouth to make popping noises at the surface of the water to let him know I was all right.

"I'm coming, Gasper!" The door flew open and Johnathon splashed in. I was so happy to see him I slapped my tail on the water.

My bowl shuddered again. Johnathon froze. The walls of the house around us groaned and shuddered. The giant fossilized toothy maw shook free from its hanger and fell, splashing down into the brown water.

"Look out!" someone outside shouted.

Sunlight appeared, bright and blindingly shining down through a hole opening up in the roof. Johnathon lunged in my direction but disappeared in a hail of falling debris as the ceiling came crashing down, throwing my bowl, and me along with it, into the darkness of the churning, muddy water.

After what seemed like forever, the rushing water in and around my bowl finally began to slow. I ardently kept myself pressed to the bottom, trying not to get swept out into dangerous waters and crushed by swirling flotsam, but the dirty water was hard to breathe and I was losing strength.

I couldn't see anything and doubted Johnathon would ever find me in this darkness.

When things were calm as they were likely to get, or at least as calm as they would get before I drowned in the muck, I began cautiously feeling along the inside of the bowl with my nose. In the murky water, the glass was invisible and I discovered the opening was no longer at the top. I panicked, thinking I was trapped in the bowl forever, and swam in desperate circles. When I tired out and regained my composure, I relaxed and just let the swirling current pull me out.

I sensed the change in the water around me signaling I was no longer within the protection of my bowl, and I pushed my way upward, toward brighter water and sunlight. I surfaced and held my mouth high, sucking in air. It helped, but it was only a temporary solution. I could only breathe this way for a little while before I would be in trouble again. I needed to find clean water and soon.

Pumping my tail, I bobbed up, turning in a circle so I could look around. I'd never seen so much water in all my life. It went as far as I could see in every direction. I wasn't even sure where I was. The town looked different from this angle. I was used to going through it with Johnathon carrying me, which placed me considerably higher in elevation than I currently was. Not to mention the collapsed buildings and water all around changed the look of the town.

An ill feeling came over me. I was looking at the ruins of Johnathon's home. Of course, it was my home as well, but I wasn't nearly attached to it as I knew Johnathon was. I thought of my bowl, lost somewhere in the murk and debris below, and discovered I was wrong. The idea of no more Sunday Luncheons with children smiling, waving, and feeding me bread crumbs left me empty inside.

Then my heart stuttered. Johnathon was under the collapsed house.

A giant splash caught me off guard and I thought I saw those giant teeth from the wall coming at me. I swam for my life, zig-zagging away from imaginary snapping jaws trying to pull me in. I couldn't see in the murk, but I raced on in a blind panic anyway, fighting my way through strange currents and eddies caused by water being in places it shouldn't.

I was yards away before I came to my senses. The splash had probably just been more of the house collapsing into the water. This muddy stuff I was swimming in couldn't possibly have any predators in it.

Could it?

The thought startled me. I hadn't needed to avoid predatory fish or birds in years. That had been a nice bonus of choosing to live with Johnathon.

I choked on silt building up in my mouth and pushed up for another gulp of straight air. As I gasped, trying to force the thin air over my gills, I tried to regain my bearings. Dark, swirling water currents pushed against me, and I fought to hold my place. I wasn't sure where I was or where to go. I needed to go back and help Johnathon.

Pushing against the current, I tried to ignore the fact I needed water—clean water—soon.

But I lived in a desert.

One currently flooded with dirty water. The irony did not escape me. One day, Johnathon and I would look back on this and laugh. If Johnathon was all right.

I ignored the thought. Johnathon and I had been through a lot together. He was resourceful and agile. He would be all right. I was sure of it.

I dove and then swam upward fast. Flipping myself completely up and out of the water, I shook off in the air, trying to clear grit from my gills. As I splashed back down I spotted two humans hurriedly wading through knee-deep water toward Johnathon's house. Gratitude flowed through me. They would help him.

"Had to be that dam they were building up north," one of them said.

"Buncha durn fools," the other agreed.

I swam back toward them. I didn't know what I could do to help, but water was my element, not Johnathon's, and if he needed help, I would do whatever I could.

Popping my head up into the air every few feet to keep on course, I was excited to see the men pulling Johnathon up from beneath broken planks of wood. I recognized the men. Roy, the older one, was a bit of a sourpuss, but he was all right. The younger one was Billy. I remembered the time he'd grabbed me by the tail and threatened to eat me to scare the girls.

I didn't like Billy much. And he had bad breath.

"I'm all right, just bruised," I heard Johnathon tell them. "I couldn't get to Gasper in time, though!"

"Just a fish. Not worth dyin' over," Roy said.

Just a fish! Ha! I'll show them! I swam as hard as I could, but Johnathon defended my honor before I could get there.

"Roy, you know better'n that! Gasper's special. She's smart. She started followin' me around like a puppy dog when I was a boy!"

"You mean you carried her 'round like a babe carries a ragdoll."

I was almost to them when something in the debris settled violently, sending waves out and nearly knocking the men over.

"We gotta get away from this," I heard Billy say as I ducked the waves. "Somebody's gonna get killed."

"I can't leave Gasper!"

My heart swelled at the words. Johnathon and I have always been close, but ever since an unusual dog named Scamp, and her equally unusual human, De, had shown Johnathon how to communicate with me, Johnathon and I have been best friends.

As I reached the humans, I launched myself up into the air, slapping my tail rapidly against the water as I went.

"Gasper!" Johnathon cried out.

"Well I'll be a sonofa—"

"We gotta find Gasper's bowl!" Johnathon interrupted Roy. "She can't live in this kind of water!"

I snapped my mouth at him, making popping sounds in agreement, but I hadn't the faintest idea where my bowl was.

"Even if you had a bowl, we ain't got no clean water," Billy said.

I don't like Billy much.

"Find me a bucket, or a jar—anything!" Johnathon began splashing back into the wreckage, pulling up boards and feeling around.

"I don't think that's safe," Billy warned.

A scream startled us all.

"Emma?" Roy turned to look. "Emma!"

Screams of terror joined with the first, both men and women's voices. I couldn't see anyone from where I was, but apparently Roy and Billy could. With worried looks on their faces, they began trying to run through the water toward the sound of the screaming.

"What the…?" Johnathon looked just as concerned but didn't follow.

I jumped high as I could, trying to see what was going on. At the apex, I managed to spot a group of humans large enough to have been most of the residents of town. They were gathered near the church, which was also surrounded by water. I couldn't stay in the air long enough to understand what they were upset about, only to see they were yelling and pointing.

Then I heard a yowl of terror that was most definitely not human. I turned and saw Charley, the miner's cat who lived in the General Store, sopping wet and clinging to a splintered post broken off from the store's collapsing awning. Her matted fur was so muddy I couldn't even make out the rings on her usually bushy tail. Although we weren't friends, my heart went out to her. Neither a creature of the day nor of the water, the flood had torn her from slumber and thrown her into both.

She cried out again, a terrible sound that told me she was scared beyond reason. She was looking to the same place the humans had been pointing.

Johnathon's voice had a tone I'd never heard before as he continued to stare toward the church. "What is that?"

Perplexed at what could distract everyone from the disaster of a flood and collapsing buildings, I jumped again, trying to see what they could see. As far as I could tell, there was nothing but swirling water where prairie had once been, but I spotted something else before I dropped back down.

Fresh water.

Slapping my tail against the water, I caught Johnathon's attention. When he looked at me, I popped my lips to tell him this was important, and then I took off at top speed for the horse trough I'd spotted. I thought I heard Johnathon splashing after me, but I needed the clean water badly enough I didn't turn around to make sure. I knew he was safe, and that was good enough. I had to take care of myself now.

On days when Johnathon carried me through the town, the General Store hadn't seemed very far away from our home, but swimming the distance against swirling, muddy floodwater felt like the longest journey of my life. I was weakening as I approached the trough. The lack of good water was catching up with me. My tail was weak and my fins felt as though the floating sand and silt had shredded them.

My nose bumped the wooden side of the horse trough and startled me. I'd gone into a daze, forcing

21

myself to continue swimming, and hadn't surfaced to take my bearings. I was lucky to have stayed on course instead of drifting off aimlessly into the murk and fading away from lack of breathable water.

The floodwater was only a couple of inches below the lip of the trough, a sizable jump to be sure, but one I could make. I jumped, already anticipating the feel of clean, fresh, breathable water flowing around my body.

I landed on the edge of the wood, hard. I knocked the bubble out of my swim bladder and gasped in pain as I fell back down into the silty floodwater.

I sank a good ways before I could pull myself together again. Without the air in my swim bladder I wasn't nearly as buoyant, and it was difficult to swim back up. I was fading. With a push of effort, I shot up out of the water as hard as I could—and found myself nowhere near the trough. I had lost my bearings again.

I quickly gulped some air to refill my swim bladder before I splashed back down, but exhaustion began to overtake me. Forcing myself on, I swam back to where I knew the fresh water was, only inches out of my reach, and tried one last time. I didn't even have the strength to get my body all the way out of the water before I began sinking again.

The taste of the floodwater was strong. Curious I hadn't noticed before. So many flavors I didn't recognize. Some tasted like plants. Others like humans. I recognized one—pickles from the giant barrel in the General Store. The children loved the pickles. I didn't much care for the salt, but the acidic vinegar was what made them too much for me. I imagined some of the other flavors were from the heard of Buffalo that had stampeded by, shaking the house down.

Wait ... that hadn't been buffalo ...

What was I doing ...?

Then Johnathon was there, cupping me in his hands and lifting me up out of the darkness.

"I gotcha, Gasper," he said as he lowered me into the gloriously clean water of the horse trough.

I tried to pop my mouth at him, but I was too tired. I tried to pump clean water over my gills, but even that was too much effort. The fresh water was good, but I faded into the darkness anyway.

The strange rumble vibrating through the water in my bowl was giving me dreams of when I'd been living in open water.

Mud! I can't breathe!

I woke thrashing my tail in terror, gills desperately pounding water through me. I could breathe, but I was blind. I couldn't see out of my bowl at all. It took me another moment to realize I was inside of the trough and looking at the featureless, dull-gray tin lining holding the water inside the wooden structure.

My panic faded as I remembered.

Johnathon had saved me.

Excited, I swam up to the surface and popped my lips to call to him if he was close enough hear. The high sides of the trough made it so I could see little more than the top of the General Store and the blue sky above me. When Johnathon didn't respond, I swam to one end of the trough and, careful not to go anywhere near the sides where I might fall out, I leapt up to get a view of what was going on around me.

I heard agitated voices and someone crying, but I found myself looking away from them. Landing, I turned and jumped the other way.

The humans were still gathered at the church, huddled up on the porch, surrounded by floodwater. If the water had retreated any, I couldn't tell. As I fell back down, I began to feel frustrated. I hadn't spotted Johnathon.

"He's gone," a raspy voice snapped from somewhere above me. "He left you. I knew he would."

I swam to the other side of the trough so I could see up to where Charley still clung to the top of the broken post. Half of the General Store was sagging in on itself but leaning away from her, so she didn't seem to be in any danger, but she didn't look good. Her fur was bristly, sticking out in odd ways as muddy water dried and caked on her.

"Humans can't be trusted when you really need them," she cursed. "Always worried about themselves first!" She adjusted her grip on the post, scooting a little higher up and then rubbing the sides of her snout on the wood to scrape drying mud from her whiskers.

"Johnathon is different!" I didn't think she would hear my protest. I didn't have much of a voice, and what little I did have wasn't made for carrying sound through the air, but she heard it.

"Sure, sure. Just like you're different from all the other fish because you're golden bright and shiny and live in a bubble. Think you're so special?" she barked at me. "He won't be back."

I stopped, stung. I had thought I was special, but I couldn't let her know that. What if she was right? What if Johnathon had left me? Anger and fear surged through me. "I'm just as special as a ring-tailed miner's cat!" I snapped back.

"I'm *not* a cat!"

I already regretted getting angry but couldn't seem to keep my words to myself. "I know that. Everyone knows that. But no one knows just exactly *what* you are! All you do is sneak around at night and scare everyone!"

Charley looked away and didn't respond. Grit in my gills scratched at my attention, so I puffed water over them, opening and closing them as hard as I could a couple of times, trying to get it out. Twisting, I checked each of my fins to see if they were torn. I was surprised to find they were fine. They felt scratched up, though.

I jumped again, trying to get an idea of what was going on with the humans. Just as I cleared the rim of the trough, I spotted something that made me forget to look for anything else. Four loose sheets of paper, covered with smeared colors and symbols, floated, ruined, on top of the brown water. The water had stained the pages and made the ink run, turning all of the beautifully drawn images into unrecognizable blotches.

Landing back in the water, I drifted, stunned. Those were the papers Scamp, De, Johnathon, and I had spent hours working on so that Johnathon and I could communicate. Even if Johnathon came back for me, we might never be able to talk to one another again.

"I'm a ringtail. I'm not a cat," Charley said quietly, startling me out of my despondency. "And I don't sneak around trying to scare everyone. I'm hunting for food."

I turned to look at her. She was looking at me with her big eyes. "I'm sorry I scared you that night. I wasn't going to eat you, I was just curious. I'd never seen a golden fish before."

"Goldfish," I corrected her. "I'm not made out of gold." I fluttered my fins self-consciously. Her words about thinking I was special still stung. Being gold colored was the reason everyone came to visit me in Johnathon's store. But the fear she was right, that Johnathon wouldn't be back, had bitten even deeper. "I didn't know you were looking for food, I'm sorry. I thought they fed you at the General Store."

"Abe used to." She looked away again and her voice grew quiet. "Before he up and left me behind."

I accidently swallowed an air bubble I was mouthing and choked. "Charley." When she didn't look at me, I repeated her name. "Charley, Abe is dead. He passed at the end of last summer."

I saw her stiffen.

"They found him out by the stream. Johnathon said he went peacefully while fishing." I didn't like to

26

think about that part, but humans seemed to think it was a good thing.

Charley's big eyes turned upward, blinking at the bright sun above us. After a long moment, her body shuddered with a deep sigh. "Just as well," she said. "He wouldn't have liked being eaten by a shark anyway."

It took a moment for her words to register.

"A shark?"

Charley nodded her head. "Yup. That's what everyone is screaming about over there. There's a shark circling the church."

"You must be mistaken. Sharks can't…" I was at a loss for words.

"Your human always says those bones up on the wall in your store, that big mouth full of teeth, came from a shark."

"Well yeah, but—"

"Well that thing swimming around out there has a whole mouth full of those teeth." She pointed in the direction of the church with her snout. "So I'd say it's a shark."

Charley stiffened, her gaze locking on something in the direction of the humans. Clumps of her fur swelled in lumps as it tried to bristle while stuck together by mud. "It's coming back!" she shrieked, scuttling up to the topmost edge of her perch.

I watched in horror, unable to see anything but Charley as she cowed. Growling low in her throat, she let loose a small but vicious roar that reminded me of a puma I'd once heard, then a giant shape appeared over the edge of the trough, leaping through the air for her. Horrible teeth snapped just below her tail as the great gray fish arced through the air and splashed back down, sending droplets of filthy water raining down into my fresh water haven.

I was knocked sideways as waves slammed into the trough. The monster leaped at Charley a second time. In spite of being off kilter, I got a better look at the beast. No doubt about it, it was a shark. One big enough eat a large human in only a bite or two.

As more muddy water splashed down upon me, I gaped in shock. I could see right through the creature. It was a ghost. It had to be. How else could a giant water-bound predator be out here in the desert?

Scamp, the unusual dog who had helped Johnathon learn to communicate with me, had said her mother hunted ghosts, when she wasn't herding sheep. I can't honestly say I'd believed the stories Scamp told, but I hadn't disregarded them either. I accepted them as something Scamp thought was real, and that was good enough for me.

I thought of those teeth coming at me in the ruins of Johnathon's house. Could it possibly be?

Charley roared again, snapping me out of my shock as the shark jumped for her a third time. The fur on Charley's tail fluttered under the shark's nose before the monster fell back to the water. The waves shook the damaged awning and rang the dangling alarm bell.

My scales constricted in fear. My nightmare had come true.

The fur on Charley's back slowly laid down and her growl quieted. Watching the direction of her gaze,

I guessed the shark had given up and swam back toward the humans. A chorus of screams confirmed my thought.

A stream of expletives, the likes I had never heard and most of which I didn't understand, erupted from Charley as she shook herself off and readjusted her grip on the post. "See if I don't!" she finished and spat in the direction of the shark.

Gunshots echoed across the water and I had to jump to see what was going on.

The church, damaged just as badly as all the other buildings, listed to one side. The humans struggled to fit on the small porch without putting themselves in danger by going into the building. The ghost shark thrashed in the water, trying to get at them. Two men were shooting while a third swung a rake at its gnashing jaws, trying to keep it away from a group of screaming children huddled at the edge of the porch.

I fell back to my little pond of safety just as I recognized that the man with the rake was Johnathon.

Now I knew why he hadn't come back. He was protecting the children. I would have done the same.

Jumping for another look, I saw the ghost shark bite at the rake and nearly pull Johnathon into the water. He wasn't going to be able to hold it off for long.

I had to do something to help Johnathon. I puffed my scales in agitation as I dodged streamers of mud floating down through my clean water, courtesy of the shark's splashing. I turned too quickly and ran into one of the murky streaks, which irritated me even more. I snorted to clear away the taste of pickles it had brought in with it. I hated that salty—

Suddenly, I got an idea.

Leaping up, I looked toward the damaged General Store and spotted what I searched for: the pickle barrel.

Knocked askew and out of its normal place just outside the door, it now stood mostly upright, wedged between the outside wall and one of the twisted poles still holding up the awning. Titled toward me, I could see it was still full of brine with pickles five times my size floating in it.

"Charley!" I called to get the miner's cat's attention—Excuse me. I mean, the ringtail's attention. "Charley!"

She turned those big soulful eyes down to me. The wet fur around them told me she'd been crying.

"I know how to save the humans!" I said. "But I need your help!"

The barking erased any last vestiges of doubt in my mind that Charley wasn't a cat. From her vantage, her voice carried clearly across the water to the church where the humans huddled together. And where the shark still circled.

"I'll give you such a what-for, you ugly tube of teeth! Come on back here and see!" Charley barked at the shark. "You sure this will work? Salt really banishes ghosts?" she quickly asked down at me.

"If what Scamp told me was true, this should work!"

Charley barked some more and then turned to me again. "What if I forget the words?"

"Don't worry. You won't."

"What if it's not enough salt?"

"Pickles are the saltiest thing I know!"

"Oh, my. It's coming back!" Charley's barks turned shrill as she edged high as she could go up the pole. "Go, Gasper," she yelled. "Go, go, go!"

I flushed one last wave of clean water across my gills and raced for the side of the trough, building up as much speed as I could, then I leaped high into the air. Up, and out, over the lip of the trough.

In my peripheral vision, I could see the shark behind me. It was so much closer than I'd expected, but it was too late to change my mind now.

As I fell to the muddy water outside the trough, I popped my lips and swished my tail to get its attention. The shark didn't notice and continued for Charley. Maybe I was too small.

Charley shrieked in terror, nearly falling off the post.

"Over here you big galoot!" I jumped again, slapping my tail as hard as I could and splashing water at the shark. That got his attention, and I got my first good look at his teeth. They were each bigger than I was. Much bigger.

And I swear they were the same ones from the wall—my nightmare lived.

I panicked and swam hard as I could. I had to get away from that monster. The muddy murk of the floodwater was worse than I remembered. I couldn't see anything. I was afraid of running into debris, but I was afraid of those teeth even more.

When I couldn't breathe the silty water anymore, I risked a trip upward for a gulp of air.

"The other way!" I heard Charley squealing as I broke the surface. "You went the wrong way!"

The shark broke the water not ten feet away as I realized I'd forgotten to follow my own plan. Hard black eyes gleamed at me and I dove back into the water wondering if all ghosts had soulless eyes. The water behind me felt cold as I adjusted my course for the pickle barrel.

There was no way I could escape this monster, but if I could just reach the barrel before it ate me, maybe I could save Johnathon. That would be good enough.

I flipped up into the air, gasping for breath as I soared. The shark erupted up behind me, moving faster than I ever could have. Only its extreme power saved me. It leaped too hard and overshot where I was already falling back to the water.

It fell back in ahead of me, its tail slicing through the water and creating eddies that sent me spinning away, disoriented and lost. Sharp grit, cut from the desert winds instead of smoothing water, filled my gills and cut at my fins and eyes. I fought the current created by the passing of the beast, trying to force myself back up to the surface to get my bearings.

I heard Charley scream before I could see what was going on. When I finally got my head out of the water, the post Charley had been sitting on was bare.

Charley was gone, and it was my fault. She had trusted me, she trusted my plan, and I … I had panicked and tried to save myself.

Swirling water caught my attention and I spotted the shark's dorsal fin heading back toward the church. Back toward Johnathon.

"No!" I shouted. "No!" That monster could not have my Johnathon. "Over here!" It continued to swim away. "Over here!" I splashed and jumped trying to get its attention.

I shouted until I couldn't see it anymore, even knowing my meager fish voice couldn't carry that far, especially in the thinness of air.

More screams came from the humans.

I choked on the gritty water. I didn't know what to do.

The smell of pickles filled my nose. I'd almost managed to get to the barrel. It just hadn't been close enough.

My strength was fading as I turned to look at the barrel, only a few feet from me now. The awning had collapsed further and, tauntingly, the barrel was tipped even farther over. I could easily jump into it myself now.

I felt like doing just that as I heard the humans scream and wondered if one of them was Johnathon. That made me wonder if Charley had suffered.

Then I noticed the alarm bell. Hanging from the falling awning, it was nearly all the way down to the water now. And the bell was a lot louder than my voice.

Maybe I could still save someone. If there was a way I could help, I had to try. All I had to do was get the ghost shark in the salty pickle juice and say the words Scamp had taught me, right?

I swam for the bell at full speed, leaped, and slapped my tail against the iron lip.

The sound was pathetic. I almost couldn't hear the bell over the wet sound of my tail slap. I tried again with no better result.

Frustrated, I slapped the water with my tail.

"Gasper? Is that you?" A timid voice came from somewhere over my head. I swam out from under the awning to see who was above me.

"Charley! You're all right!"

"It almost got me!" Charley hung her nose over the edge of the tilted roof and looked down at me, her eyes big and scared. "I made the biggest jump of my life to get here! And look!" She turned and showed me the bare pink tip of her tail where ringed fur was missing.

"I've got to save the humans," I said, "but I can't ring the bell. Can you do it?"

Her eyes widened, something I didn't think was possible, and she backed away. "No! No, no, no!"

"Just ring the bell, and then get back up there where the shark can't see you. I'll do the rest. I promise I won't mess up this time."

An extra loud scream from the humans punctuated my plea.

"Please Charley. I can't do it alone."

"Just one ring?"

"Just one!" I agreed.

Charley leaned over the edge and examined the bell, looking for a way to come down. I choked on some grit and spit it out, trying to ignore my fading energy from lack of clean water.

"Okay," Charley agreed, and then she climbed down onto the bell. With front paws hooked on the awning, she pushed the bell with her back legs, slowly rocking it back and forth.

"Good job," I told her. "You can do this."

Pushing and gaining momentum, she continued until the clapper finally struck and rung. And then she pushed again, ringing the bell again, and again.

"You did it!" I cried.

"This time we're gonna get that—"

The bell clap covered her words, but I was sure I knew what she meant.

Charley climbed back up on the roof of the awning and stood on her hind legs, looking out toward the church. "Be ready, Gasper! It's coming fast this time!"

"Tell me when to go," I said.

"Ready…"

I took a gulp of pure air and puffed my scales.

"… set …"

I was ready. The ghost shark didn't have a chance this time.

"… go! Go, Gasper, go!"

Trusting Charley, I leaped from the water next to the bell, slapping my tail and making all the noise I could to get the ghost's attention. I saw it surface just as I fell back down. When I felt the pressure of the water it pushed ahead of itself, I leaped again, as far as I could go.

The ghost shark leaped after me and I could feel its coldness catching up with me. The barrel was only a little more than one more leap away. I could do this. Teeth gnashed in the water behind me. I skimmed up to the surface to see where the barrel was. My timing had to be perfect for a jump like this.

I flipped my tail as hard as I could, lifting myself up into the air just as I felt the void of the shark's dagger-riddled jaws upon me. At the last possible instant, I drug my tail, the friction against the water dropping me right back down and bringing me to a dead stop.

The shark, anticipating my jump, followed the arc I would have made and landed headfirst, jamming its oversized snout into the pickle barrel.

I started trying to chant the words Scamp had taught me, but I was too out of breath. They came out broken and stuttered.

The shark thrashed and pickles and brine sloshed out through its ghostly body.

Somehow my words got stronger, louder than I'd ever been able to speak. They weren't just my words. They were Charley's, too. As we spoke in unison, the ghost fought to free itself from the barrel, rolling and splashing all around.

And then an even stronger voice joined in.

Johnathon appeared next to me, chanting the same words. He must have learned them from De.

The ghost shark managed one last mighty flip of its tail, spinning the whole barrel around before the power of the words overtook it. There was a bright flash, and I thought I saw something swimming up toward the sky, and then the ghost was gone.

Johnathon held a cigar tin down low to the water and motioned for me to jump in. I wasn't crazy about cigars, but I trusted Johnathon, so I jumped.

The relief was instant and blissful. Later Johnathon told me it was holy water.

The fire crackled in our new pot-bellied stove. I dozed as I watched it from my new crystal bowl. The sun was setting and the coming night was chill. Our new store had been finished last week, just in time for the fall weather.

Charley's nose peeked out of the box Johnathon had made for her and placed by the stove so it would stay warm. She waggled her whiskers at me and headed straight to the bowl of food Johnathon put out for her. After a quick sniff and a smile of approval, she stood on her back legs and pointed at the framed newspaper hanging on the wall. With a quick wink and a smile, she headed out to search for prey, just to keep up her skills. At least that's what she said when she went out last night.

I looked back to the newspaper on the wall. It had an image of me, Charley, and Johnathon all together under the headline *Town Heroes*. I liked looking at it. It made me happy.

A knock on the door woke me just as I was about to fall asleep. It was a little late for visitors.

"Coming!" Johnathon came out from the back room and answered the door. "Billy! Come on in." Johnathon held the door open.

"Look what I found." Billy stepped in, holding up the fossilized jaws that had once hung on our store wall.

I don't like Billy much. At least if those jaws come alive again, I know I'm the fish for the job, and I'll have Charley here to help me.

The End

A Colorado native, Sam Knight spent ten years in California's wine country before returning to the Rockies. When asked if he misses California, he gets a wistful look in his eyes and replies he misses the green mountains in the winter, but he is glad to be back home.

As well as being Distribution Manager for WordFire Press, he is Senior Editor for Villainous Press and the author of five children's books, three short story collections, two novels, and nearly three dozen short stories, including two media tie-ins co-authored with Kevin J. Anderson.

A stay-at-home father, Sam attempts to be a full-time writer, but there are only so many hours left in a day after kids. Once upon a time, he was known to quote books the way some people quote movies, but now he claims having a family has made him forgetful, as a survival adaptation. He can be found at SamKnight.com and contacted at sam@samknight.com.

Sam Knight

BROWN AND THE ALLOSAURUS WRECKS

BY J. A. CAMPBELL

Como Bluffs, Wyoming 1901

Elliott, my human and I, had come to the Dino Dude ranch to put another dangerous specter to rest. If I could herd my first dude while we were at it, even better. They had a ghost problem and I was the dog for the job.

I'd herded cows and sheep before, but never dudes. I didn't even know what a dude was, or a dino for that matter.

Elliott climbed down from the wagon when an older man approached us.

"Mr. Gyles, thank you so much for coming. It's...it's terrible." The man who greeted us smelled bitter and salty, the reek of exhaustion. He pumped Elliott's hand and smiled. "I'm Curt Gummer."

"Please, call me Elliott. Dino Dude Ranch, huh?"

Curt scuffed the ground with his foot. "Well, I ain't no paleontologist or anything, but I listen.

41

Learned a few things. Got enough knowledge to impress the dudes anyway."

My ears perked. It sounded like they had more than one dude to herd.

"You know more than I do on the subject."

"Well, you know more about ghosts than I do. I tried getting a priest out here. He wouldn't come and recommended you."

Elliott's scent shifted to surprise. "Well, Brown is the real mastermind behind the ghost hunting operation. She catches them. I banish them."

"I hope she likes big ghosts. Let's see to your horses and get you put up, then I'll show you around."

We trailed after Curt. The hard packed dirt held dry, deserty scents, but I smelled water too and the dusty hay smell of cows. I perked my ears and looked around. Nothing was better than rolling in cow pies, except maybe herding sheep and fighting ghosts.

Prairie grasses rippled in the slight breeze, lining the bare dirt path we walked on. Scrub brush led to actual trees in some places. Fencing held back a few cows and I saw ridges and exposed cliffs in the distance.

Elliott patted his thigh and I trotted up to his side. We walked past corrals, some with horses eating hay. Our horses nickered greetings when they saw the others.

"I've set aside a cabin for you and your dog, Brown, is it? Unoriginal name for a brown dog, isn't it?

"I was annoyed with her at the time I named her. She was eight weeks old and had chased the entire herd of sheep into a ravine. It took a full day to get them all out."

"Ahh, well." He smiled down at me and winked, whispering 'good dog.' Out loud he said, "The horses can have that corral there. The hand will make sure they stay fed and watered. You can park your wagon by your cabin. Meals are served in the main lodge there." Curt pointed to a large stone and wood building not far from our smaller wooden cabin.

"It sure is pretty out here. Those ridges really add to the scenery," Elliott said when we stopped.

"Yep. That's where the dino bones are, too. Scientists say they're the Morrison, Sundance and Cloverly formations. Jurassic era or some such. Got huge dinosaurs, some of them meat eaters, fish, all sorts of fun things, if you like old bones." Curt shrugged. "They're pretty interesting, but I really like that it brings the tourists." He grinned and rubbed his fingers together in a motion I'd seen people use to refer to money.

"How exactly did an operation like this get started? Though it's kind of a new thing, I've heard of people paying to pretend to be cowboys, but not paleontologists." Curiosity colored Elliott's scent.

Curt glanced around as if telling him a big secret. "I followed the prospectors out here during the Bone Wars."

Elliott's scent shifted to confusion.

"You know, all those folks fighting over dinosaur bones 'bout twenty some years back? Well, when that dried up, I got some of the land. Heard about other ventures, guided hunts, and all that. Figured why not guided bone digs, and, well, occasionally I host a scientist or two, but mostly just folks with money from back east. Doesn't hurt that they can keep the bones if they can transport them." Curt grinned.

"So, these ghosts, do you know what they are? Old prospectors?" Elliott turned the horses so that they backed the wagon up against the side of the cabin.

"Bigger 'en that," Curt answered.

While he unhitched the horses, I sniffed around the cabin. An interesting scent caught my attention and I stuck my nose in a crack where the wall of the cabin touched the ground.

"Hello?" I inhaled the fresh odor.

"Hey, get your slobbery nose out of here."

I jumped back and tilted my head before creeping forward again. "Who are you?"

"Said, git!" A pair of eyes gleamed in the shaft of light.

"Sorry." Working my nose, I tested his scent. Smelled like raccoon. I'd barked at many a pest such as those in my time, but since this one wasn't doing anything, I backed off and continued my exploration.

"What!" Elliott shouted.

Jerking my attention from the interesting scents, I dashed toward Elliott's side, hackles up and ready to fight whatever had upset him.

"Yep. They're dinosaur ghosts. One of them, paleontologist called it an allosaurus, is a big old meat eater. The scientists loved it, said they could learn so much about how they actually move and hunt. 'Course then it chased one of the scientists into a gulch. Broke his leg clean through the skin. No matter how interesting something is, if it's huge and acts like it wants to eat you...people leave. We've got some vegetation eaters too. Guess this place used to be pretty lush, all those years ago." Curt scratched his head. "Thought I'd told you they were dinosaur ghosts."

"No, I believe I would have remembered that."

"Ahh." Curt shrugged. "Well, we got dinosaurs. Bones and ghosts of 'em. I kinda like the ghosts, but, well, I can't live on grass like the cows can. A few folks came out to see the ghosts at first, but after that scientist got hurt, people were scared. Last one said it looked him in the eyes like it could see him straight to his soul. That was enough. He told everyone he could think of and no more money for me. Think you can get rid of 'em?"

Calming, since Elliott didn't seem to be in danger, I sat and studied the humans. Curt stood with shoulders hunched, eyes slightly widened and eyebrows raised. Elliott's eyebrows were also raised, but his shoulders were thrown back.

"I...have no idea."

"Welp, give it a try. No hard feelings if you can't." Curt patted one of the horses on the shoulder and took its lead from Elliott. "Help you with these two, then I imagine you're hungry. We'll get to the ghosts soon enough." He led the horse toward the corral and Elliott, shaking his head, followed.

Elliott opened the corral gate and turned the horse out. "Many ghosts can interact with the physical world, but they're usually angry ghosts with business that keeps them from moving on. I can't imagine what business a dinosaur might have. Maybe the ghosts are harmless."

"Hmm, hadn't thought of that." Curt let the other horse loose and they both kicked up their heels before settling in to munch on hay. "Maybe we can take a cow out there where the ghosts are and see what happens. If it doesn't kill the cow, then we've got ourselves a safe attraction. If not, well, at least we know."

"Brown can herd a cow out for you, if that's what you want to do."

Curt looked over at me before nodding. "It's a plan."

The cow walked calmly in front of me as I pushed it with my border collie Eye, out to where Curt said the dinosaur ghosts normally congregated. I enjoyed herding the cow, but it wasn't making my work difficult and I longed for a challenge. It would be so easy to sneak forward and nip it. Just get it moving a little faster, but I refrained. Even though this cow was boring, Elliott trusted me to do my job properly.

We wound around some scrub brush and I got to dart forward and push the cow along when it tried to eat a tuft of grass. Jaw dropping in a doggy grin, I quickly wagged my tail, before settling back into work.

After a short time, the main ranch buildings disappeared behind a rise as we went down into a bowl. I smelled water.

The cow mooed, possibly also smelling the water. It was puppy play to get it to step out from the meager cover of the scrub brush and give it a push.

"That'll do, Brown," Elliott called once the cow was well on its way to the small stream that ran through middle of the bowl.

I trotted back to Elliott's side and we settled in behind a rock.

"How long does it usually take them to appear?" Elliott looked around.

Curt shrugged. "Seems to vary."

"You've never seen them anywhere else?"

"Sure. But they always start here. I've seen 'em get as far as the ranch before they vanish."

"And they've never hurt anyone?"

"Thing is, they're kinda slow. A sprinting man can outrun the allosaurus. The paleontologists were surprised by that. We think it's because he's a ghost. He certainly looks like he can run a lot faster."

"So everyone has managed to run away."

Curt kicked the dirt. "So far."

Elliott took off his hat and spun it around in his hand, before putting it back on. His scent soured to nervousness.

"Hmm, what's that?" Curt crawled around the rock, staring at something in the clearing.

"Curt, maybe later…"

"Naw, don't think the dinosaurs are actually dangerous. Besides, that smooth rock looks like an egg. I can make money off of those, too. The scientists said so. I just prefer not to do my own prospecting." Rising to a crouch, he glanced around before running out into the clearing. Once he got there, he knelt near the cow and picked something up.

I wanted to ask what a dinosaur was, and why they were so afraid of them. Unfortunately, humans didn't understand animal speech. So far all Curt had talked about was bones and eggs.

"Damn. Just a rock." He threw it back to the ground.

The cow mooed.

The air chilled and the sun dimmed. Elliott gasped and I followed his gaze upward. The creature looked something like a giant roadrunner I'd seen once, except with a blunted nose, partially blocked the sun. I could see sky through its translucent body, though it took up more of the sky than any animal I'd ever looked at, even the elephant at the zoo I'd gone to once. I tucked my tail.

Ghost scent—the sharp scent that came after a rain, but musty and old like a moldy cellar—hit me. Elliott called it musty ozone. This ghost smelled a little different. Its scent also made me think of damp, rotting plants. I wrinkled my nose, but I didn't dart forward to try and herd this ghost as I normally would have. Instead I sank to the ground at Elliott's feet, not sure I could fight something like that.

Curt froze.

"That's a..." Elliott trailed off.

"Shh, it can hear. That's the allosaurus. Don't move," Curt whispered and gestured for us to stay back.

It moved on two legs, leaning forward and swinging its head back and forth. The cow mooed nervously and trotted away. Curt ran the other direction, past the ghost. It swung its muzzle as Curt ran past, catching him with the side of its massive head. Curt screamed and went flying through the air.

Mooing frantically, the cow bolted. The huge creature picked up speed and chased the cow, perhaps thinking it would come back for Curt later as he didn't move when he hit the ground.

Elliott swore quietly and rose to a crouch. "We can't just leave him," he muttered. "Not dangerous my…" the last was said with a growl.

The cow tangled in some scrub, slowing it just enough that the ghost caught up. It gaped its jaws wide and snapped them shut on the cow, cutting its frantic moo off abruptly.

The ghost lifted the cow into the air, shaking it, and ripped flesh. The body fell to the ground. The metallic scent of blood carried on the breeze.

As soon as the ghost was distracted by its meal, Curt scrambled to his feet and ran back toward us, eyes wide, scent reeking of terror.

Elliott tugged on my ruff and dragged me away once Curt caught up to us.

The ghost tore into the cow, ripping, bone-crunching sounds warring with the hot smell of blood overwhelming my senses.

Elliott stopped abruptly and we stared as a four-legged ghost with a neck longer than a tree and an equally long tail lumbered past. It bit at scrub, tearing some up, before continuing on its way.

"The strange thing is," Curt whispered, "they eat real plants but don't leave footprints."

"So, what do we do?" Curt joined us on the porch of our cabin a few hours later, limping slightly.

I lay with my head on my paws, enjoying the scents the breeze brought to my nose. I still wanted to find a cow pie, but for now I was content to sit while Elliott studied his books for a solution to the dinosaur ghost problem. A partially chewed bone from my dinner lay next to me. Once I finished sniffing, I'd tackle the bone again.

My nose twitched. I caught the musky scent of the raccoon that lived under our cabin. I scooted until I could see over the side of the porch. He pushed his way out of the hole in the side boards and looked up at me, little nose twitching.

Meanwhile, Elliott explained how we normally hunted ghosts to Curt.

"Usually I draw a circle on the ground, with some symbols that trap ghosts. Brown uses her border collie Eye to herd the ghost into the trap, and I dispel it with a Latin incantation."

"Hmm, sounds complicated."

"We've worked out the kinks in the system." Elliott's chair creaked as he leaned back. "But this is entirely different. From what I understand from my grandpappy's journal, the Latin speaks to something in the ghosts that probably won't work on a dinosaur. They predate the language after all. I can't imagine I'll find unbroken ground big enough to make a circle to contain that allosaurus, either. The circle, even if it would work, has to be unbroken, or it won't hold a ghost."

"I see your problem. So, no Latin and no circles. You got anything else?" Curt sat down on another bench.

I turned my attention back to the raccoon. He sniffed the ground. Impulsively, I nosed the bone off the porch and it fell in front of the raccoon.

He jumped back and hissed at me, but when he saw what I'd offered, he quieted and tilted his head. Resting my muzzle on my paws, I watched. He walked forward and, after a quick sniff, snatched the bone and dragged it back under the cabin.

Licking a little drool from my lips, I turned my attention back to Elliott. He'd get me another bone.

"Might be able to find some bones, or something else the creature is tied to. If we can get the ghost to the bones and destroy them, it might work." Elliott paused between words, worry lines creasing his brow. "That's a lot of ground to cover."

Curt sighed. "Guess we can start looking, first light." Curt stood and clomped down the stairs.

The sun faded completely and Elliott turned up the wick on an oil lamp to continue reading.

"Looks like you've got a problem, Dog." The raccoon came out from under the cabin.

"The locals have a problem," I replied. "I'm here to try and fix it. My name is Brown."

"My name is Azeban. A visitor called me that, so I took it as my name. Thanks for the bone."

"You're welcome." It occurred to me that I still didn't know what a dude was, though I'd discovered what dinosaurs were. Maybe Azeban knew. "Azeban, what's a dude?"

The raccoon stared at me, whiskers twitching. "What?"

"This is a dude ranch. They must ranch dudes, like cattle or sheep. So far I haven't seen one, but I would like to herd one. What is it?"

Azeban laughed, rolling over on his back, paws twitching in his mirth.

"What?" Huffing, I laid my muzzle on my paws, ears flat.

"A dude ranch is where humans come from the East and pretend to be cowboys. Or in this case, scientists. They're called dudes."

"Dudes are...people?"

"Yes." Azeban laughed harder.

Well that was no fun. I wasn't allowed to herd people. Grunting and feeling dumb, I changed the subject. "What do you know about the dinosaur ghosts?"

Azeban's laughter died and his hair stood on end. "They're big, stinky, and stay away from the cabins, so I stay over here."

"We need to get rid of them."

"What's this we, Dog?" The raccoon hopped back a few steps.

"Elliott and I need to get rid of them. Curt will probably help, too. I can't see what a raccoon would do, anyway."

Azaban wrinkled his lips at me and dashed under the cabin.

"Come on, Brown. Let's get some rest. We've got bones to dig up tomorrow," Elliott said.

Wagging my tail, I dropped my jaw in a doggy grin and followed Elliott inside. I liked bones and digging. Tomorrow would be fun.

"You're sure you know what the bones look like?" Elliott leaned back and wiped his brow with a cloth, leaving smears of dirt.

I watched perched on a rock. I'd helped dig for a long time, but we weren't getting anywhere, so I'd lain down. The one bone I'd found smelled like a rock and I hadn't wanted to chew it.

"I'm sure. We've got some back in our museum, that a paleontologist left for us. Wasn't good enough for a museum."

Elliott stopped and stared at Curt. "Wait...what did you say?"

"We've got a skull and a few leg bones back in the museum. Hardly a complete skeleton, but enough."

"Of an allosaurus?"

"Yep." Curt's eyes widened. "Oh."

Elliott sighed. "As much fun as digging is for Brown, I don't enjoy it all that much. Did the ghosts happen to appear around the time you uncovered that set of bones?"

Curt scratched his head and shrugged. "Thereabouts."

"Right. Let's go look at those bones." Elliott stood and shouldered the shovel he carried.

"Sure, good idea." Curt sounded like he'd tuck his tail between his legs if he had one.

I trotted ahead and the two humans trudged behind. As we skirted around the low bowl the wind shifted, bringing a familiar swampy scent.

My hackles rose as I turned. Growling, I crouched, ready to defend my humans, though I tucked my tail and wanted to run.

The allosaurus loomed behind us. Its mouth gaped open, exposing translucent teeth bigger than the steak bones I'd enjoyed the night before. Elliott twisted around, shouted and threw his shovel at the ghost. Curt dropped his and sprinted toward the ranch.

"Brown, run!" Elliott raced past me.

The ghost ignored the shovel and stared at me, crouching, nostrils flaring as it scented the air. It took a step forward and I held my ground. I had to give Elliott time to get away.

"Run!"

The creature darted forward and I dodged, trying to catch its eye. I didn't know if I could control it, like I could other ghosts, but I would try.

It looked at me. There, I got its eye with mine. I caught its mind! Just like a human ghost. This felt very strange though. I held it still for a moment. I could herd these ghosts!

It wrenched out of my control, roaring.

The sound blasted around me. I yelped, tail tucked.

I'd given Elliott enough time. As the ghost lunged forward, I turned and sprinted for the ranch.

Once I caught up to my human, I stayed at his side, but we managed to leave the dinosaur behind.

"See what I mean," Curt gasped, when they collapsed onto the porch of the main ranch house. "Runs like it's in molasses. Sure am glad, too."

"I bet it was fast when it was alive." Elliott lay back, panting.

I found a good patch of shade and rested while the humans recovered. The run barely winded me, so I watched for the ghost, making sure it hadn't followed.

"I'm surprised the ghost doesn't come over here, if it's tied to the bones in your collection," Elliott said after a few minutes.

Curt shrugged. "You complaining?"

"No, but that might mean we have to find something else before we can destroy it." Elliott sat up.

"In that valley? I'm not going in there."

"How much dynamite do you have?" Elliott scrambled to his feet and held his hand out for Curt.

"Plenty." Curt let Elliott pull him up.

"All right. We'll try and destroy the bones and the ghost first. If that doesn't work, Brown and I will see if we can find the rest."

"Wait, those bones are valuable. We can't just destroy them."

"You agreed last night." Elliott crossed his arms.

"Yeah, when it wasn't my private collection."

"Your private collection isn't going to do you any good if you're dead."

Curt sighed. "True. All right, let's go have a look."

He led us into the main ranch house and through the dining area. I licked a little drool from my lips at the meaty stew scent that came from behind the kitchen doors.

The back of the house was full of bones. I walked up to one and sniffed, but it was those stupid rock bones that were no good for chewing. Huffing, I sank down on the floor and watched while Elliott inspected the pieces Curt showed him.

"That's all of it. Skull, a few leg fragments and one vertebrae."

"Brown, come here and sniff these. Do they smell like the ghost?"

Tilting my head, I wondered how bones could smell like a ghost, but I came over and applied my nose to the rocks Elliott held. Strangely, I thought I did catch a hint of swamp and musty ghost scent.

Wagging my tail, I sniffed the other pieces and woofed.

"Think we've found our bones. I just hope they're enough. Too bad it's not a complete skeleton." Elliott looked at Curt.

Curt shook his head. "I swear it's all there. I want the ghost gone, too. Anything else is still buried, or destroyed by time."

"Okay. Now we need a good place that we can catch the ghost."

"Big old pit, not far from its territory. We can put the bones and dynamite there. We'll have to go around the back of the ridge. Don't want to attract the beast while we're working. Think we can lure it in with another cow?" Curt winced.

"Let's get the pit set up, then we'll get a cow out there, and see what we can do." Elliott touched the skull again.

"Take most of the day to get a wagon over there. Maybe we should start out at first light tomorrow."

"It's a plan." Elliott clapped Curt on the shoulder.

"What are you doing, Brown?" The raccoon came out from under the porch.

"We're going to defeat the dinosaur ghost." I glanced over to Elliott. He and Curt worked on getting the last of the bones into Curt's wagon.

"How?" Azeban asked.

"We're going to get it to come with that cow." Curt had a cow tied to the back of the wagon. "Then we're going to put it in the pit with the bones and blow it up."

"Interesting." The raccoon followed when I trotted over to Elliott's side. He stayed back, but watched while Elliott scratched my ears.

Curt paid the raccoon no mind, but Elliott studied it.

"He's friendly," Curt said, without looking.

I wagged my tail when Elliott glanced at me.

Elliott nodded to Azeban, and climbed onto the wagon. Curt joined him. I took up position behind the cow to keep it moving.

This cow, if anything, was more boring than the last. It didn't need any encouragement to follow the wagon. When we reached our destination, Curt untied the lead rope from the wagon. I expected it to try and bolt. Instead, it put its head down where it stood and tore at the grass.

Huffing, I flopped to the ground and stared at the cow.

"What's so interesting about the cow?" Azeban crouched down next to me.

"Nothing." I grunted.

"Then why are you staring at it?"

"It's my job to make sure it stays put."

The raccoon laughed. "You're doing a fine job."

Ignoring Azeban, I rolled over on my back and wiggled around, enjoying the dust. If the cow was going to be boring, I could at least have a good roll.

"Okay, Curt, get the cow out into the bowl."

"What, isn't that why you have your fancy dog?" Curt stared at Elliott.

"These are your ghosts. I'm not risking her."

Curt glared.

Elliott crossed his arms.

Sighing, Curt tugged on the lead, but the cow wouldn't budge.

"Hah!" I said to the raccoon. "See, I was helping."

Azeban snorted.

Curt pulled with all his might, but the cow refused to budge.

I wasn't afraid of any ghost, even a dinosaur. Before Elliott could tell me to stay, I darted forward, nipping at the cow's heels and pushing the cow toward the bowl where the dinosaurs roamed.

It mooed nervously as we crossed into the creature's territory.

"Brown, be careful."

The swampy ghost smell strengthened and the cow tried to bolt. I jumped in front of it and stopped it from running.

Curt dropped the lead and ran.

The swampy ghost smell grew stronger and I heard the dinosaur roar, but I still didn't see it.

"Brown!" Azeban shouted.

My nose had deceived me! The ghost raced up from the side.

Curt screamed and changed direction. Roaring, the ghost darted its head forward. Its jaws clamped shut around Curt's middle, blood spraying. Curt's scream cut off abruptly as the dinosaur shook his head back and forth.

"Brown, run!" Elliott yelled.

The dinosaur wouldn't make it to the pit if I didn't move the cow. We couldn't let it get away, not if it was going to kill people. That ghost had to be stopped.

Ignoring Elliott, I dove in, snapping at the cow. Between my prodding and the approaching ghost, the cow ran. I made it go toward the pit. The dinosaur kept it moving.

The cow faltered when it saw the pit ahead, but I grabbed its heel with my teeth and it leapt forward. I'd never purposefully driven any stock off a cliff—even a small one—before. I didn't care for it, but I knew the plan.

The cow mooed from the pit, and I dodged around the rim, but the dinosaur's attention stayed focused on me.

I faltered, not wanting to lead it back to Elliott, but not sure what to do. I looked back. Its mouth gaped wide. I dove to the side, just as it struck. The dinosaur's ghostly jaw seemed to sink into the ground right where I'd been standing.

Yelping, I bolted away from the ghost. The ground fell away from my feet before I saw the pit in my path.

The cow mooed and scrambled away from me as I tumbled to the rocky ground.

"Brown, watch out!" Elliott shouted.

The dinosaur leapt to the ground next to me, teeth snapping shut a whisker's length from my tail. Ghost scent washed over me, filling the pit with its reek.

I ran for the edge of the pit, hoping it would chase the cow instead so I could escape.

It chased me.

I turned when I got to the edge of the pit, knowing I couldn't climb out fast enough.

Suddenly, a shiny light played across its face, distracting it. I bolted between its legs.

The cow mooed again.

The dinosaur roared and the moo cut off abruptly.

"It's got the cow, get out, Brown!" Elliott's voice rose, cracking when he sobbed my name.

I leapt at the side of the pit, clawing at the loose rock.

Elliott threw himself down at the edge of the pit and grabbed my scruff. He dragged me out as I scrabbled at the dirt. We tumbled backward, Elliott holding me tight.

"It's going to escape!" Elliott scrambled to his feet.

I couldn't let it leave the pit. It would catch Elliott! My Eye had worked for moments before. Maybe it would be long enough to keep it in place while Elliott destroyed it. I dashed to the edge of the pit, barking frantically.

I watched as it swung around toward me, bits of cow dangling from its jaws.

It met my eyes, huge teeth bared.

I grabbed it with my Eye. The dinosaur froze, but it fought me.

"Hold it, Brown." Elliott shouted in the language he used to banish ghosts.

The ghost fought against me. My grip on its mind weakened. Its tail twitched like a cat's.

"Brown, behind the rock!" Elliott grabbed my scruff and dove for the ground, just as the loudest noise I'd ever heard blasted my ears.

Yelping, I cowered behind the rock as dust and rocks sprayed from the pit. Gravel rained down around me and I leaned against the Elliott. Dust covered my fur and I cowered, not certain if it was safe to move.

Azeban scuttled over to me. "Brown, are you okay?" His voice sounded tiny, and far away.

"I think so." I scrambled to my feet and shook the dust from my coat.

Elliott stood went to the edge of the pit, and peered into the obscuring dust cloud.

"I sure hope that worked," Elliott said.

The roar in my ears dimmed. His voice sounded more normal to me.

Elliott dropped to his knees and wrapped his arms around me, pulling me close.

The breeze carried away the dust revealing nothing left in the pit except rocks.

"I guess we'll have to go make sure it doesn't come back." Elliott eyed the bowl where the dinosaurs came from, scent sour.

Elliott led the way and Azeban and I followed. I was certain Elliott had destroyed the ghost. He never failed. We all dodged sideways around a piece of what had been Curt. Hackles rising, I whined. Azeban scuttled around to my other side.

Elliott sighed and put his hat to his chest for a moment. "Too bad. I kind of liked him."

Turning my attention away from the remains, I looked at Azeban. "I sure am glad that light distracted the dinosaur. I thought it was going to eat me."

"This light?" The raccoon sat back on his hind legs and waved his hand. Light shone on Elliott's back for a moment, before Azeban fell to all fours again.

"That was you?"

Azeban chittered, sounding pleased. "Me and my shiny." He held out his paw and showed me a bit of mirror.

"Thank you." I wagged my tail. "You saved my life."

"You're welcome. Thanks for helping with the ghost. It gets boring without the tourists around to throw me interesting food."

We crept into the bowl and though we watched for it, the allosaurus didn't appear, though we did see the plant-eating dinosaurs.

Elliott stopped in the center of the bowl and leaned against a pile of rocks, fear scent easing. "Guess we got it."

I woofed agreement.

"Brown, these rocks are shaped strangely. Almost like an egg. I like eggs." Azeban touched one of the rocks so I went up and sniffed it.

Smelled like a rock to me.

"What did you find, Brown?" Elliott knelt next to me and brushed some dirt off the rock. "Is that?" He hesitated, "Eggs. Maybe that dinosaur wasn't a he after all. If she were protecting her eggs...Too bad Curt isn't around to claim them. Maybe it would have made his fortune." Elliott ran his hand along the smooth shapes for a moment.

"Oh well. Good dog, Brown." He ruffled my ears. "Another ghost sent back to where it belongs. I guess we can leave the others, though." He glanced up and we watched one of the long necked dinosaurs lumber past. "I think they'll leave us alone."

Wagging my tail, I touched noses briefly with Azeban before leaning against Elliott's leg, looking forward to the next job. If someone called with a ghost problem, I was the dog for the job. I just hoped the next ghost wouldn't be able to eat a whole cow.

The End

When J. A. Campbell is not writing she's often out riding horses, or working sheep with her dogs. She lives in Colorado with her three cats, Kira and Bran, her border collies, her Traveler, Triska, and her Irish Sailor. She is the author of many Vampire and Ghost-Hunting Dog stories the Tales of the Travelers series, and many other young adult books. She's a member of the Horror Writers Association and the Dog Writers of America Association and the editor for Story Emporium fiction magazine. Find out more at www.writerjacampbell.com.

KOTORI AND THE DEMONS

BY LAURA HARGIS

It was hot today. But then again, it is always hot in the desert. Thankfully, heat doesn't bother me much. I'd been born here in the desert. I wandered slowly across the sands, moving from one shade source to another, in no particular hurry. We had no place to be, so, we just wandered.

My name is Kotori, and I am a Donkey. Some say I have been *Spirit Touched* by the great owl spirit Mongwa. I know this is true, because my human, Ahote, told me so. He found me in the desert when I was very young. My mother had been killed by a *toho* — or mountain lion, but I was small enough that I hid in a crack in the rocks, so the *toho* could not get to me. But Ahote did. When he found me he took me home. He gave me food, water, and a name. He called me Kotori, which means Screech Owl Spirit, it suits me, because...

HEEEEE-HAAAAAWWWWWW!!!!!!!!!

"Kotori!" Laughed Ahote. "My screeching owl!"

Ahote and I were in no hurry today. We had already taken care of the demons that plagued the Hopi people for so long. Now, Mongwa said to head north. This is why we are out in the desert. Traveling north through the New Mexico territory, working our way up toward the new state of Colorado. There is a lot of nothing out here, but if Mongwa wants us to go this way, there must be a reason.

"Kotori, we should start thinking about finding a place to get out of the Taawa's sight for the day," Ahote said, shading his eyes as he looked up at the sky. He watched as Taawa, the sun, was heading toward the peak of his travel across the sky. "Taawa will be hitting his peak soon. I think we should find somewhere shady, hopefully with some good water for us to drink."

I didn't mind the heat much, but the hottest part of the day could be bad for us. I picked up my pace a bit and trotted toward a large grouping of rocks that looked promising, it helped that I could smell water from that direction. I liked the rocks. They provided good hiding places, and if there was water there, there might be something green to eat. These rocks were also tall enough to block out the heat that Taawa gave during the day, providing some needed shade. So, that is where I went.

I liked trotting across the sands. My hooves were hard and made for this type of terrain. Ahote's horse, Takala, while a very nice horse, doesn't do well in the desert. She has good, hard feet, but she can't handle the heat the way I can. So, when Taawa is at his peak, we stop.

As I got close to the rocks, I found an opening between two of them. They created a nice ring around a spring, with a few over hanging rocks near the top to provide some shade. There was even grass around the spring, and Ahote was pleased. "This is a good spot you picked for us, my friend," he said.

Haaaww...hee haw, hee haw

"I'm glad you agree with me little one." Ahote laughed. He liked that I understood what he said. Takala could too, but she didn't talk as much as I did. "Yes, this is a good place indeed," he said as he got down off of Takala, loosening her girth and removing her bridle. He didn't usually hobble or tie either of us, we wouldn't leave him. After seeing to Takala, he came over and removed the packs from my back. We didn't need much as we traveled. Ahote was a good hunter, and the Spirits provided for us as well. As long as we had fresh water, we would be ok. Takala carried Ahote, and I carried the things we couldn't find along the way. As soon as he finished with me, I followed Takala to the water to have a nice, long drink.

"Hey! Leave some for me!" Ahote called. As if Takala and I could drink all this water ourselves.

After drinking my fill, I wandered around nibbling at the grass, lost in thought, when...

"Watch out long ears!"

Looking down, I noticed a small lizard in the grass, near my nose. "Sorry, I didn't see you."

"Obviously!" The lizard ran through the grass and up on a rock. "Why don't you look where you're going?"

"I didn't expect to find a lizard in the grass. Normally, you would be on a rock, sunning yourself." I wandered over so I was eye to eye with the lizard. He was a beautiful Collared Lizard, with white spots over his dark brown body, and a black and white collar around his neck. "What were you doing in the grass?"

"Well, how else am I supposed to get to the water?" He walked right to the edge of the rock and looked at me. "What are you doing out here anyway?"

"Mongwa told Ahote and me to head north, so we are heading north."

"Mongwa, eh?" The lizard looked around me to where Ahote laid things out for his afternoon rest; Takala grazed nearby. "What would Mongwa want with you?"

I turned my right shoulder to the lizard, "You see that marking on my shoulder, at the end of my stripe?" I turned back to face the lizard. "Mongwa marked me, so I could destroy demons. We go where Mongwa tells us to."

"That is an interesting mark, almost looks like a feather," the lizard said, looking over my shoulder. "I guess if Mongwa said to go north, you must go north." He turned and ran to another spot on the rock. "Doesn't give you an excuse to nearly eat me though!"

"I wouldn't eat you! I only eat grass." But the lizard wasn't listening any more. He'd gone to another part of the rock and was sunning himself. "As if I would eat a lizard. Gross!" I mumbled as turned and went back to eating, watching carefully for any more lizards.

As Ahote rode Takala along the open road, I trotted along exploring all the plants that grew in this area. Ahote told me when we crossed into Colorado, but it looked the same to me; dry, sparse and hot. It didn't take long, however, for things to change. The grasses became taller, and greener, than the desert, and instead of short scrubby bushes, there were tall trees. Taller than I'd ever seen.

Shortly after we'd crossed into Colorado, Mongwa had visited Ahote in a dream and told him we were to head to a place known as Idaho Springs; a large mining colony in the mountains of Colorado. He told Ahote the workers were being plagued by demons. It would take us more than a week to get there, and while I was enjoying the grass and trees around us, I worried we would be too late. From what Ahote had said, the workers were having a terrible time with the demons.

It had been closer to two weeks to make the trek to Idaho Springs. The mountains were steep and finding a path that Takala could easily follow proved harder than we'd thought. Ahote said it was a good thing it was summer, otherwise, we'd never have made it over those mountains. When we arrived in Idaho Springs, Ahote found a good place to camp, near something called the Argo tunnel. He told me it wasn't a mine really, but a tunnel being built to connect several mines, to help in removing the water that builds up in the mines. However, before the tunnel could be finished, the work had stopped. There was something in the tunnel that was scaring the workers.

After setting up camp near the river, we climbed the hill to the tunnel construction site where Ahote went looking for the foreman. He tied Takala to a hitching post, but left me loose, as always. As I walked around looking at things, trying to figure out what might be going on, a little man sitting on a rock, caught my eye. He seemed to be watching me, so I walked closer.

He looked to be no taller than my leg, but was wearing miner's clothes. I wondered at first if he might be a child, since he was so small, but children don't normally have full beards. As I stared at him, wondering who, or what, he was, he spoke to me.

"Well, what are ya lookin' at?" he said to me. His accent was strange, something I'd never heard before. I looked around, wondering if he was actually talking to me or not. No one actually talked to me, other than Ahote. People tended to talk at me, but never to me.

"Cat gotch'er tongue? I asked ya simple question." He jumped down off his rock and walked over to me. The top of his miner's hat was level with my chest, and as he got closer he reached up to the mark on my right shoulder. "Well, now. That's somethin', make no mistake." He said, stepping back to look at me directly. "You'd think with a mark like that, you'd be smart enough to talk to me. Since I know you kin see me."

"Um," I started.

"Well, maybe not that smart after all." He started to turn away.

"I am smart!" I stomped my foot. I didn't like being called dumb.

"Well, then...what d'ya know. You can talk!" He skipped around and clapped his hands. He was a strange little fellow. Now that he was closer, I could also see that he appeared to have a slight, greenish tinge to his skin.

"Of course, I can." I said, wondering about this strange little man. "My name is Kotori. What's yours?" I asked, being polite. Everyone should be polite, that's what Ahote always said.

"Me names, Tristin," said the little man. "Whatcha be doin' here? You who has been touched."

"My friend Ahote and I are here to take care of the demons," I said. Looking again at the little man's green skin, I tilted my head and eyed him closely "...are you a demon?"

He laughed heartily, and I almost brayed out loud, laughing with him. "No," he said when he'd caught his breath, "but there are many a miner who'd call me that." He laughed more as I tilted my head to the left and looked at him funny. "I'm known as a Tommyknocker 'round these parts. My people live in the mines and tunnels round here. We help the miners when we can. Warn 'em of danger and the like."

"Have you seen demons here?" I asked. I was still trying to understand what a *Tommyknocker* was.

71

"Oh, aye, I have. Devilish creatures, chased even me brethren outa the tunnel they did!" Tristin started stomping his feet and shaking his fists. Then, just disappeared! I looked all around for him, but he was nowhere in sight. Ahote, however, now stood next to me.

"Well, my little friend," he said as he came up beside me. "Seems there's been some little guys around here who've gone bad. The Miners call them Tommyknockers, and say they are usually very helpful, but for the past month, they've been causing damage and even a few deaths in the tunnel." Ahote stroked my neck as he looked at the tunnel entrance. "Seems there is more than one, so I think you have your work cut out for you."

I stood there, thinking about what little Tristin said. He *was* a Tommyknocker, but he said there were also demons here. How was I going to explain that to Ahote? That the Tommyknockers weren't the ones causing the problems. Did it matter? If I got rid of the demons, the Tommyknockers could go back to helping the miners just as they had before. I figured that was good enough for now. Besides, there was no way I could tell Ahote so that he would understand.

I trotted back to the camp, with Ahote running along behind me. He made himself dinner while Takala and I ate grain and more grass. I liked the grass here in the mountains of Colorado. It was tall and lush and very tasty! Not like the short grasses that grew in the desert. As I was wandering around grazing, I saw Tristin again. "Hello." I said as I walked over to him.

"Been wonderin' Kotori," he said, hoping up on a rock so we were the same height, "how do you plan on dealin' with them demons?"

"Well," I said, "when I bray, really loud and long, for some reason, they seem to freeze. Then, while they are frozen, I go up and kick them in the chest, hard, with both hind feet. That destroys them, and they vanish."

Tristin scratched his chin, or his beard, I couldn't tell which.

"I suppose, seein's how ya are spirit touched an all, that jus' may work." He stopped scratching and looked at me. "Have you done this before?"

"Yes." I nodded. "Many times. Ahote and I got rid of the demons that were bothering the Hopi nation. We would find them, then I would freeze, and kick them. Ahote then does something with sage that keeps them from coming back."

"Aha!" Tristin jumped. "That makes sense. You need something that will keep the evil from returning."

"That's what Ahote says." I turned my head to look back at Ahote. He didn't seem to notice Tristin standing there, or that I was talking to him. "He also said that the miners and workers think you are what is causing all the trouble in the tunnel."

"They would." Tristin huffed. "Silly humans, they ain't ne'er seen a demon, but if somethin' happens in the mines that ain't good, 'tis us they be blamin'!"

"There's no way for me to let Ahote know it isn't you. But I think if I get rid of the demons, that's all that matters, right?" I looked at the little man.

"Aye, that should' be doin' it, alright." Tristin's face lit up as he thought about it.

"How many demons are there, anyway?" I asked.

"Hmmm, now...lemme think." Tristin tapped his head a few times, "I think we seen at least 3."

"Three!?" I cried. I must have let out a *hee haw* as well, because Ahote came over.

"What's the matter little one?" He asked when he got to me. I butted my head into his side as he reached over and scratched behind my ears. "What's got you worked up?"

"Do'na worry, he can'na see me." Tristin did a little dance on the rock. I let out another *haw...hee haw, hee haw*, in laughter at his dance.

"Silly donkey." Ahote scratched my withers and went back to his camp fire.

"So, silly donkey," Tristin mimicked Ahote, "Ya worried about three demons?"

"Well," I hesitated, lowering my head a little

"I see ya are." He folded his arms across his chest. "What's the problem? Have ya ever takin' on that many before?"

"Not all at once, no." I wiggled my long ears in thought. "I had to deal with two of them at once, and that was hard enough. The second one was coming out of the effects of my bray by the time I got to it." I laid my ears back alongside my neck and shook my head in memory. "It almost got me!" I shivered, remembering those claws coming dangerously close to my legs as I kicked.

"Well, then, we'll jus' haveta think o' a way to keep you safe then." And with that, Tristin popped out and was gone.

I blinked and shook my head, wondering, if he wasn't a demon, how he could just disappear like that? But he didn't feel like demon, so he probably wasn't. I tried not to think about it much as I headed back to Ahote and the fire. I lay down near the fire, and tucked my head back along my side, thinking I would get some sleep. Takala came over and lay down next to me. Ahote laughed, seeing us both laying there by the fire, "You two didn't leave me much room." It might be summer, but in the mountains, it could get cold at night. Ahote spread his blanket across the fire from us, piled on a little more wood, then he too lay down.

At about midnight, as the moon was highest in the sky, I awoke. I brought my head up and swiveled my ears to try and catch whatever sound it was that caused me to wake up. I looked at both Takala and Ahote, but they still slept. Then I heard it: "psst." The sound was like air escaping a tea pot, just before it started to whistle. Swiveling my ears, I found the direction of the noise. As I turned to look that way, I saw Tristin. He waved his hand at me, calling me to him. I carefully got up, trying not to disturb Takala or Ahote and walked over to where he was.

"My brothers and I have a solution to yer problem." He said, when I got to him. "When do ya plan on dealin' with them demons?"

"Ahote said we'd be going into the tunnel in the morning."

"Good. My brothers will be there with ya. After ya freeze the demons, as they start comin' to, we'll distract 'em. That should give you time to freeze them again." He smiled.

"That might work." I said.

We stood there discussing ways for Tristan and the other Tommyknockers to distract the demons; dropping rocks down on their heads if they could get above them, tripping them with rope, things like that. As we talked, a large owl came down and landed on a tree branch above us. I looked up and knew it was Mongwa. I couldn't tell you how I knew, probably had something to do with him being a spirit that helped me recognize him. I bowed my head in greeting.

"Kotori." The voice spoke more in my head then aloud.

Tristin jumped and turned to face the owl. "Saints alive!"

"Tristin, this is Mongwa, the owl spirit." I pointed my nose up at the owl.

"Ya were no kiddin' when ya said yer doin' his work!" Tristin removed his hat and bowed to Mongwa. "Good even m'lord."

Mongwa tilted his head, as owls do, to Tristin. "Spirit of the mines, I appreciate you helping my Kotori in this task, but you must be warned. As a spirit yourself, you and your brothers will be paralyzed by Kotori's call. You will not be able to help him."

"Well now, I dinna think of that." Tristin scratched his beard again, thinking.

"What else can I do, Mongwa?" I said, "I don't think I can take on 3 demons at once."

"The only way the mine spirits can help you is if they cannot hear you. If they are too close when you paralyze the demons, they too will be paralyzed." Mongwa blinked his large owl eyes. Then spreading his great wings, he took flight, leaving Tristin and I there alone.

"This changes things," Tristin said, then popped out of sight again. I walked back over to the fire, and carefully lay down, wondering how I was going to get rid of three demons. Before I knew it, I was asleep again.

The next morning, after a breakfast of a little more grain, Ahote gathered the things he would need for banishing the demons together. He left Takala hobbled at the camp so she wouldn't follow us. He needed her for riding, but she couldn't help with the demons. When all was ready, we walked back up the hill to the tunnel entrance. As we got closer, we saw the foreman and a few workers standing not far from the entrance. Ahote walked over to them.

"Good morning, gentleman," he said as he neared the group. "Are you ready for us to start this morning?"

The foreman looked over at Ahote, he had a puzzled look on his face. "Well, I suppose so." He turned around again, looking at the boxes before them, "seems the Tommyknockers were about again this morning. That, or the mice are getting stronger."

"What do you mean?" Ahote looked around the foreman at the box. I did as well. There were several boxes stacked near the entrance. The lid had been removed from the top box and it was sitting on the ground next to the stack. The open box appeared to have several bottles in it that looked like they may have been packed with cotton. But most of the cotton seemed to be missing now, except for a few pieces that had been dropped on the ground near the lid.

"Don't make no sense," said one of the workers. "This here box of nitroglycerin was all packed carefully with cotton. But this morning, the lid is off, and most of the cotton has been removed. Without disturbing a single bottle of nitro!"

Haw, hee haw, hee haw, hee haw I laughed. I knew where the cotton had gone! The Tommyknockers indeed! They had figured out how to make themselves deaf! Ahote looked at me sideways. "What are you laughing at?" I just shook my head and walked to the tunnel entrance. Time to get to work.

I walked in first, as I always did. Ahote would come in behind me, after he lit the sage. But we didn't want the smoke too close to the demons before I could destroy them. The further I went in the tunnel, the cooler and dimmer it became. Deep in the mountain, away from the sun the tunnel stays cooler and darker. One thing about a tunnel or cave, with the mountain wrapped around you like a great big blanket, the temperature doesn't change much, and this time of year, it was cooler than the outside air. I stopped long enough for my eyes to adjust to the light, then noticed, along the upper walls, several Tommyknockers. They were waiting for me, their ears overflowing with cotton. I found Tristin, and he smiled, and pointed to his ears, and then started forward into the tunnel. I nodded and followed.

The workers had been working on the tunnel for about 2 years now, according to Ahote, and they had gotten quite a ways in. As I walked down the tunnel, I felt the air grow warmer and there was a bad smell. Ahote had called it sulfur and said it was something the demons caused. With those two clues, I knew we were getting close. I stopped and waited, and I could hear Ahote stumble behind me somewhere. He never carried lamp with him, he said it would alert the demons. I didn't think it mattered, the demons always knew we were there. I was thinking about going back to help him, when I saw the first demon. It was large; larger than any demon I had dealt with before, with big red eyes and a forked tail. Its feet were like those of a goat, but it still had claws for hands. Those claws made me shiver just thinking about the time I almost got too close to one. Then, more movement. There were not two more behind it, but three! Four demons! I was sure glad there were so many Tommyknockers there! These demons were bigger than any I had faced before as well. I would have a hard time kicking them in the chest, in just the right spot to destroy them! They were so tall!

I took a deep breath, then;

HEEEEE HAAAAWWWWWW!!!!!! I let out the loudest, longest bray ever! It echoed in the tunnel, causing a few small rocks to dislodge and come down on Ahote and me. But the demons stood, frozen in place.

I trotted up to the first one, looking at how tall he was. Figured the only thing I could do was rear up on my hind legs and strike out at him with my front feet. My tiny front hooves hit him hard, right in the chest. But he didn't explode as the other demons had. No, instead, he fell over. I got around him so I could aim my kick just right, the kicked as hard as I could. That worked! He exploded into a million pieces, like dust scattering when the wind blows suddenly. But just as he exploded, the other three demons freed themselves and started toward me.

Tristin and his brothers swarmed the demons, yelling and banging their little hammers against the hard hats, making a terrible racket! Even Ahote covered his ears. The demons ignored me and went after the Tommyknockers. Some of the Tommyknockers stood up on ledges, throwing rocks down at the demons, while others tried to get a rope pulled across the tunnel to trip the demons. The demons got close to Tommyknockers several times, and I was worried for their safety. I knew I had to stun them again. So, I took another deep breath and…

HEEEEEEHAAAAAWWWWWWW!!!!
HEEEEEEEE HAAAAWWWWWWW!!!!

I let out two brays! I don't know if it would work any better, but I wanted to make sure the demons were stopped. And they were! Unfortunately, that time, so were a few of the Tommyknockers that had lost some cotton while distracting the demons. I couldn't worry about them at the moment, I had to dispatch the next demon. This one wasn't quit as large as the first, and as I got closer, I knew I'd only need one kick. So, I turned, got into position and fired off with both back feet, as hard as I could! That demon exploded in cloud of dust as well. I ran to the next demon, it wasn't yet free, but I could see the clawed fingers starting to move. I had to be fast. I turned and again, fired both back feet as hard as I could. The demon exploded. Only one left, but when I faced him, he moved. He was free.

As I was getting ready to let out another bray, the demon vanished. The Tommyknockers all looked around at one another, and then they too disappeared. I slowly looked around, wondering where the last demon went, then I saw.

Ahote. He stood stock still, his eyes red and glowing. The demon had gone into Ahote!

What was I going to do? I couldn't kick Ahote! If I kicked him as hard as I did to destroy the demons, I would kill him. He was my friend. I didn't care how badly I wanted to destroy the demon, I couldn't risk anything happening to Ahote.

"Ah, so you do care for this human," the demon said, using Ahote's voice!

"Get out of there, demon!" I pawed the ground and tossed my head, hoping to scare him.

"You won't hurt me, not while I'm in here. I think I'll just wait until my brothers are back, then we'll destroy you all. You, this man, the tunnel workers, and those bothersome little spirits that live here!" He laughed, and although it was Ahote's voice, it was the scariest thing I'd ever heard. Ahote didn't laugh that way.

As I was wondering what to do, I felt a slight tug on my ear. Tristin appeared, sitting on my neck. "Kotori, use your bray. It will free Ahote. Trust me!"

Then he disappeared. I wasn't sure it would work, but I had no choice. I took a deep breath…

"I wouldn't do that if I were you." Said the demon in Ahote. "You will kill this human."

HEEEEEE HAAAAAAAWWWWWWW!!!!!!!!

I brayed so loud and so long that more rocks fell from above. I hoped none would fall on Ahote and hurt him, but as I finished braying, I saw several of the Tommyknockers appear, and push Ahote over, while several others caught him before he hit the ground. And left standing where Ahote had been, was the last demon! I ran up, turned and kicked as hard as I could, causing him to explode in cloud of dust. Ahote sneezed, because he was so close that time, but it helped bring him to his senses. He scrambled over onto his hands and knees, and found the glowing sage stick. Carefully standing up, he began chanting and waving the sage around. The demons would never be back.

As we came out of the tunnel, the foreman ran up to us. "What happened in there? We thought the tunnel was going to collapse on you!"

"Well, there were a few times that I thought it was as well," Ahote said, brushing as much tunnel dust off of himself as he could. "But, you have nothing to worry about anymore. The demons are gone."

"Um, not that I doubt you, but how can I be sure?" The foreman asked.

"Walk into the tunnel. You'll see for yourself," Ahote said, putting out the last of the sage stick. He didn't want to waste any of it.

The foreman pointed to three men, and the four of them cautiously walked into the tunnel. After about 30 minutes or so, they came back out, smiling. "The tunnel is clear men! Nothing bothered us, and the heat is gone!" The foreman yelled.

"Hurray!!!!" All the workers yelled.

"I can't thank you enough, Ahote. Kotori." The foreman said. Then he handed Ahote a small bag. "I think this might help though. All the mine owners got together and decided if you could get rid of those pesky Tommyknockers, they wanted you to have this."

Ahote took the bag and put it in his pouch with the sage stick. "Well, I hate to tell you this, but you still have Tommyknockers. They weren't your problem," Ahote said, looking down at me. "Yes, I saw them, and felt them when they knocked me down." He rubbed my ears as he turned back to the foreman. "You did have at least 4 real demons, though. The Tommyknockers helped us get rid of them. So, I would keep them happy if I were you. They will let you know if there are any more problems in that tunnel."

"And if there are any more problems?" The foreman asked.

Haw! Hee Haw! Hee Haw! Hee Haw! I brayed.

"I agree Kotori. Just call us. Kotori is the demon hunting donkey for the job."

The End

Laura has worn many hats over the years. She was a paramedic in the San Francisco Bay Area for several years before changing careers to become a 911 dispatcher in her home town in Lake County California. After moving to Colorado in 1994, she found another hat...that of technical writer and quality engineer for medical device design and manufacturing companies. She had her first book published late in 2016, a coffee table holiday book called A Friesian Christmas. This is the first of a series of *Horsey Holidays* books that are planned for release.

Laura and her family live in a small town on the plains in Colorado with her dog Belle, and her horse Dani. While there are no plans to get a demon hunting donkey, She's sure if one showed up with a feather pattern on his shoulder, he would find a home with her and her family. You can learn more about the *Horsey Holidays* at giftedwithwords.net

HARBINGER

BY CAROL HIGHTSHOE

I perched on the branch nearest the entrance to the interior of the great oak. The first part of the storm was passing and the eye would soon be here. I could already sense fear growing throughout the area. Souls disturbed by the storm and needing guidance. We would have to move swiftly during the relative calm of the eye to find them all.

Other members of the clan began exiting the oak, stretching their wings and waiting. Most of us had taken shelter in the ancient oak growing in the center of the oldest section of the cemetery. The magic that was part of this place protected the oak and it protected us.

The winds slowed, light filtered through the clouds, and I saw others coming to join us. I trilled, calling everyone together, and the others, here at the oak, joined the call. Any humans who saw us would probably panic at the sight of so many of us in one place. They would be right to do so; but not for the reasons they believed.

Humans have long associated us with death—believing if they heard us call three times it meant we were calling their soul and they would soon die. The truth is, when we issue the spirit call it is because the soul has told us they will be leaving the mortal body and we are binding ourselves to the soul so we can locate and guide them across the veil to their next existence. We are not the harbingers of death; we are the guides to the next life. For those who are not ready to pass through the veil, we guide the souls to safe and protected places until they are finally ready to pass through or fade away.

The storm finally broke and the eye was on us. As one we took to the air beginning our search. This storm was one of the strongest to hit the area in many life times and we all felt the pain and fear in the spirits who had been disturbed. On silent wings we split apart and begin our search of the cemetery. We would first find and assist those already in our charge. Then we would begin our search for the lost ones—souls who died suddenly and were not bound to a guardian or guide. Souls unable to pass beyond the veil because of the circumstances of their death. These were the ones we, and others like us, would be searching for during the days after the storm passed.

Soon the air filled with the spirit call as members of the clan located wandering spirits and lost ones then guided them to safety. I found myself drawn toward the main building of the Eternal Escapes cemetery. The pain and fear I felt almost overwhelmed me. I beat my wings furiously, fighting against the strengthening storm winds desperate to reach the building. I soon had several other members of the clan flying with me.

I could sense a deep darkness, radiating from the building. Unseen by normal eyes, it was something created from the depths of despair, anger, pain and loneliness. But, in the midst of the darkness there was also a bright soul: Lieke, the current director of Eternal Escapes. To mortal eyes it only appeared she might have fainted or only laid down on the carpeted floor of her office. But, to my eyes and sense, her soul was being drawn from her body toward a shifting smoking form made of darkness. Her soul called out to me. As soon as the spirit call flowed from my throat I felt the magic shift slightly. Where the song normally wove a thread of power between myself and the spirit this was more like a net being cast. A blanket, warm and protective to surround the soul and guard it. A shield to prevent the darkness from continuing to drain Lieke's soul from her.

The others who flew with me joined in the call and we could 'see' the magic surrounding Lieke's soul with a golden light—like a shield. Once again the darkness reached out to engulf her. The shield flared and the darkness retreated, but only for a moment.

I could 'see' Lieke's body on the floor; a thin tendril of light still connected her soul to her body— she wasn't dead. At least not yet. Hearing other members of the clan gliding through the air I called them to this place. It had been many generations since we had to fight one of the devourer—the magic of the cemetery normally keeping them from passing into this world. Was it the storm that weakened the wards? Or was it something on this side that called the devourer through.

As more of the clan arrived I could sense the shield around Lieke's soul strengthening. But, as long as it remained separated from her body there was nothing Lieke could do to stop the devourer. Looking through the window, I saw one of the older ritual books laying open on the director's desk. Had Lieke been the one to summon the devourer? That made no sense. She was a guardian and a guide—just as the members of my clan were.

The wind continued to build as the eye of the storm passed and the second band hit the area. I heard several squawks from younger members of the clan as the power of the storm surprised them. Careful to maintain my connection to Lieke's soul, I directed everyone to the roof of the building. It was seldom used, but there was an opening there designed to allow members of the clan to enter the building. A secondary roost to protect us when needed.

Once we were all inside, I moved to the small door that opened to the director's office. Lieke's soul was still connected to her body. A good sign. The acoustics and insulation of the building prevented outside noises from penetrating the offices, but now that the clan was inside and the small door open, the sound of our song resonated throughout the roost and the director's office. The darkness that was the devourer turned toward the opening and shrank back as I stepped through.

Stretching my senses, I touched the darkness. This was *not* a demon, as I originally suspected. This was a lost one—a soul that had been wandering for generations. Fear had made it a devourer—fear of passing on—fear of fading. I glided to the open ritual book and glanced at the page. It was a ritual of binding—similar to the spirit call. It would have bound this lost soul to Lieke until it could be guided beyond the veil. The director had a pure, unblemished soul, and in trying to help the lost one, she had opened too much of herself. The devourer had been unable to resist drawing her soul into itself; as it had others over the centuries it existed.

Glancing at the lost one then at the ritual book and Lieke, I made a decision. With a sudden sharp trill, I broke the spirit binding I had with Lieke and focused on the lost one. If I was wrong I could lose not only my own soul, but Lieke's as well. As I sang the spirit call a shimmering silver light surrounded the lost one, binding us together.

Several other members of the clan came through the opening—my mate gliding to land next to Lieke's body. She began trilling a different song—one that would call Lieke's soul back to her body. I could hear others in the roost joining her song.

I continued binding the lost one to me and felt the darkness pulling at my soul. I wanted to flee but instead began strengthening the bond and drawing the darkness away from the lost one. Projecting safety and hope into my song I focused on the soul before me and ignored the chill growing in my body. Others joined with songs of hope and peace. The darkness surrounding the lost one began fading. Slowly at first as its fear continued to fight us. Then, finally the fear lost its hold and I felt hope replacing it.

The storm continued to rage outside. Wind and rain pounded the building and thunder shook the windows. I led the lost one to the fountain in the atrium of the building. Perching on the upraised arm of the Archangel Raphael I carefully opened the veil. The lost one hesitated for a moment as indecision and fear again rose up around it. I nodded and blinked my eyes slowly as I watched. I could only guide and open the pathway; I could not force.

A green sparkle surrounded the figure of Raphael as a peaceful silence filled the area erasing the sounds of the storm. Softly, almost like a gentle caress, I could hear a song of hope coming from the other side of the veil. As the soul passed through, I heard a whispered "thank you" then the veil closed.

I brushed my cheek against Raphael's marble one and sighed softly. The chill from the darkness that touched my soul was colder than any freezing rain I had ever been caught in. But, now warmth flowed from the figure of the Archangel to chase the final vestiges of the devourer away. With a trill of thanks, I silently winged my way back to the director's office.

Lieke's soul had rejoined her body and she now sat at her desk; the ritual book closed. My mate was still with her and Lieke absentmindedly stroking her feathers. I heard murmuring and the rustle of feathers coming from the roost as the clan settled down to wait out the remainder of the storm before returning to our duties as guides and guardians for the souls of those we were entrusted to protect.

The End

Carol Hightshoe was an avid reader at a young age. Her strong desire to write came from her love of (her husband calls it obsession with) Star Trek. It was this early love of Star Trek that led her to the Science Fiction and Fantasy genres.

Carol currently edits and publishes the online e-magazine: The Lorelei Signal. She also runs a small press publishing company: WolfSinger Publications, works full time and is a published author. Her books include *Call of Chaos, Chaos Embraced, The Road Into Chaos and Chaos Challenged.* In addition to numerous contributions to different anthologies she has also edited several different anthologies.

You can visit her online at www.carolhightshoe.com

Carol Hightshoe

FERRY HORSE

BY J.D. HARRISON

Sage kicked up from under my hooves, and my nostrils wrinkled in warning only seconds before I sneezed so hard my forelock flopped into my eyes. Shaking my head in disgust, I plodded onward, driven by the compulsion that carried me to my next job.

How I hated sage, and cactus, and yucca and every other thing about this forsaken desert. What I wouldn't give to get back to the good old days, when I picked up fallen knights on the battlefields of England and France. Or even during the War between the States, I could usually find a nice meadow to take a break in. At least in between jobs I could relax in the deep green fields of juicy grass. Here in Arizona, things were dry at the best of times and utterly inedible at the worst.

Still, I'd gotten good at finding the watering holes where you could crop a few mouthfuls of the good stuff. Even now, my mouth watered at the memory of the rich, succulent blades, juicy on my tongue as my teeth ground together at the phantom memory.

Caught up in the thought, the next sneeze caught me by surprise. Twisting my neck, I bit at the air in objection as if the scents were no better than a fly buzzing around my head. Not that it would help, but for a second, it felt good to indulge in the urge. My job of collecting souls didn't give a lot of time to be selfish, and sometimes I envied the mustang bands I occasionally saw. Sure, they lived a harsh life hunting for food and water, keeping away from predators, but no one told them where to go or what to do all the time.

When Death had greeted me, I could have chosen the peace of Elysium, where the grass grew ever green. But I had been so horribly young, and sure of my own strength, wanting the earth beneath my hooves and the wind in my mane. Endless years later, I couldn't even recall when I had last galloped for my own enjoyment.

I heaved a longsuffering sigh, then sought some sort of silver lining before my temper frayed even more. For one thing, I didn't have to carry a saddle like most horses. Nor bridle either. Most folks never really saw me, just a mirage passing in the distance. Well, unless they were dead.

Which lead me to where I was headed now. The magnetic pull had grown stronger, and if I lifted my head to look down my nose so I could see into the distance, the telltale glow of a soul in need of a ride winked at me. Sadly, it came from a darker blot of

94

buildings on the horizon, and I wrinkled my lips in distaste.

Why couldn't it have been a native? They were always so simple, and you've never met a more respectful people when it came to horses. Then, it was awe and gratitude, with a light seat on my back as we galloped through the veil that carried us to the other side. Even some cowboys were tolerable, having made their living with my mortal brethren, and appreciative of their works. But most townies weren't so pleasant, treating me like a vaguely sentient bicycle. And have you seen those ridiculous things? Unnatural, if you ask me, balancing on two wheels. Why anyone would prefer that to a horse who knew the way home was beyond me.

Dusk calmed some of the unrelenting sun as I drew near the town, which made the glow a bit easier to pick out. I'd expected to be visiting the cemetery on the outskirts of all the buildings, but no, the glow shown steadily from the crossroads of two main streets. I headed straight up the middle of the wide main thoroughfare, unafraid of being seen by the humans moving about. To them, I was a faint breeze, maybe some motes of dust that wove between them with a bit of warmth.

Still, that didn't stop the animals from noticing. A cat walking on the porch in front of the general store arched its back and puffed its tail, and a group of dogs in the alley by the hotel barked a warning. The horses all gave way, a few lowering their heads respectfully as I passed. They knew me for what I was, a horse meant to ferry the dead, a job any of them could choose once they left this life. Once they shed their mortality, the curtain was open to them as it was to me. Only humans needed help to pass through.

One colt barely under saddle shied away at the light I emitted, while the older gelding cast him a wide-eyed look of surprise. Clearly, the youngster had a lot to learn about the world. The light grew stronger as I neared my goal, and I shook myself all over, shedding the dust from my pearlescent coat so I would shine. First impressions were everything, and a little bit of awe usually kept folks more respectful.

As I rounded a cluster of humans emitting an unease that made my skin shiver, my target came into view, and for the first time in many years, surprise widened my eyes. The tall cowboy I had come for sat with purposeful negligence in a worn rocking chair, sitting beside a younger man still very much alive. Between the pair sat a saggy faced hound with a gaze just as sharp as the soul I was tasked to retrieve, both of them scanning the street and ignoring me completely.

I stamped my hoof impatiently, and snorted hard enough to ruffle the hem of the young man's chaps, making him sit up in alarm. Wide eyes hunted for the source of the gust, but skated right over the space where I stood. His hand made it halfway to his revolver before he visibly shook himself and settled back in his chair, faking a calm he in no way felt. The kid stank of fear, but I recognized the honorable resolve in his eyes that meant someday I'd be tasked to carry him, too. Soon, if the thick tension in the air were any indication.

"Well, big horse, that weren't too kind of you. Poor Gus is already jumpier than a long-tailed cat at a barn dance, no need to rile him up any further."

I turned my attention toward the soul, giving him a better inspection now that I had his attention. Lean as a desert cougar, and just as dangerous, the man studied me in return. I noticed the dog mimicked him exactly, though the canine raised his lip in offer of aggression while the no longer mortal human remained placid.

"I imagine you've come to take me to my reward." The cowboy drawled, but rather than rise, he sank deeper into his chair, the coat he wore gapping open to reveal a sheriff's star that emitted as much light as the rest of him. Usually, such things would be dull to my eyes, a mere shadow of the man he had once been, but clearly, the star was part of the fabric of him.

My brows wrinkled in contemplation as we examined each other, and I decided to break my usual silence. Perhaps this soul was a cut above. "I'd be grateful if you would mount up, sir, so we can make a quick journey and we can both be about our business."

Dark amusement filled the lawman's smile. "There, we shall have to disagree, big horse. I've got business that keeps me here. Until I see the outlaw in my jail properly hung, and his ghost exorcised to its own judgement, I'm holding the watch. Gus is too green to do this on his own, and I made an oath to this town to keep them safe."

At the word oath, his whole incorporeal form pulsed with the light of conviction. Recognizing the strength of his belief, I knew even if I carried him, he would not pass through the veil. Unfinished business made for ghosts, and that would leave a man clearly deserving of the other side quite stranded. My own sense of responsibility felt like the heaviest of yokes for a moment, and I bowed my head at the weight.

"You've no power to influence the world anymore, lawman," I said wearily, nostrils pinched against the truths I had to tell him. While truly honorable men were rare, they were also among my toughest fares. Their ties to the world were strong indeed, either for love, loyalty or duty. Asking them to cut their ties and find freedom was never easy. "Leave the mortals to their follies, and take the rest you've earned."

This time, the cowboy snorted. My head flew up as the kid eagerly shot to his feet, looking toward the door of the jail as if expecting someone to emerge. Clearly, the sheriff at least still held sway with the young man, and if the glare the hound delivered was any indication, with the dog as well.

The kid had slumped back into his chair with a sigh of disappointment before the lawman addressed me again. "Bear with me, big horse. The trial is the day after tomorrow, if the townsfolk can hold off on lynching him, and they'll hang him shortly after. Once he's shuffled off, I can chase his ghost off proper like, and we can get wherever you're needin' to take me. Not long, in the great scheme of eternity, I'd think."

Indeed, what was a few days compared to infinity? But to deviate from my duties chafed like an old saddle sore that my mortal form had once worn, making my tail switch with impatience. "I can give you time to see him dispatched, lawman, but you'll have no power over him in death unless you are also a ghost. You are an itinerant spirit, meant for traveling to the afterlife, not a shiftless ghost."

The man suddenly leaned forward, elbows to his knees as his phantom bootheels thunked against the wooden porch, inaudible to human ears. Yet, as the soul assessed me with a flint hard gaze, the kid spooked like the green colt as the vibration traveled his direction. "You mean to say I'm not going to get the pleasure of delivering the justice this man is owed? He's bled this town of money, goods, and people for years, and I won't let him continue to plague them in the afterlife."

"No sir, I'm afraid that is now beyond your control. But I've a suggestion, should you be concerned about a vengeful haunt."

His eyes widened in surprise as he sat back and steepled his fingers, exuding a patient watchfulness that I could appreciate. While no longer a mortal equine, I still possessed the same instincts as my brethren, happy to coexist with anyone that wore such a deeply rooted peaceful awareness. In my earthly years, I would have been proud to carry a human like him on my back, whatever work we faced. Old memories made the skin over my withers shiver, my mane waving in a phantom breeze as I recalled racing into battle with my companion at arms. But I shook them away, much as I had the dust I'd worn earlier, and focused on the present.

"If we could find a way to send a message to Miller, Colorado, that would be fastest. A telegraph, I believe you call them."

The hound dog cocked his head to the side in contemplation, a gesture that seemed quite popular among canines. His mental voice was incredibly clear, with bell like undertones that made my ears twist. "I might know a source."

Then he shot from the porch despite a yelp of objection from the young man, no more than a blur of black and tan on the darkening street. The lawman stared after his dog with a baffled twist to his lips until the animal faded from sight. "Talking animals. I'll be stuffed."

His eyes eventually sought a fresh target, and for several silent moments he looked blankly into the distance, which bothered me not in the least. Horses liked quiet, after all, and I cocked one hindleg to stand hipshot. Things would come together or not, and I'd take the developments as they came.

A mere fraction of my long life passed before he refocused on me, and mustered a tired smile. "Well, big horse, if we're going to be keeping company with each other, I'd like to be mannerly about it. I'm Cole McInnis, sheriff of this little town. How should I address you?"

I curled my neck slightly so I could better study him with one eye, turning both ears to focus on this continuously surprising man. "It has been decades since anyone cared to know, Sheriff. But if you like, you may call me Aube."

"Aube?" Cole echoed, a question clearly in his voice as he studied me with a horseman's eye.

The crest of my neck tightened as I tossed my head. My form and color had made me much admired from birth, as the sun rose up and lit my still wet body on a cool spring morning. "They named me for the dawn."

"I'm sure you catch the light like a jewel," Cole conceded, pushing to his feet. He stood quite tall, even without the assistance of the porch, though I imagined my muscular girth would fill the length of his leg. "And I'm sure things will stay quiet up here long enough for me to offer you some hospitality. We should get you off the street. Can't believe no one's come up to wrangle you yet."

My ears flattened out to the sides. "None of them can see me, Sheriff. I'm as much spirit as you. No need for hay or water, though I'm known to enjoy the occasional mouthful of grass, or the chill of spring water down my throat. Sleep is of little concern, though I find a sandy wallow still gives some pleasure."

"You're a'tween as me, then?" He jumped down beside me without disturbing so much as a mote of dust, and while his hand lifted as if to stroke my neck, I appreciated when he curbed the gesture. We weren't familiar, though I imagined it wouldn't take long before I could welcome his touch.

I nodded, an affectation picked up from the humans I'd studied over the centuries. "I chose this, though. Which gives me a bit more play than one like yourself, still adrift. My purpose is to ferry the deserving to the afterlife, anyone either innocent or neutral, or rarely, the honorable."

Further conversation halted, overshadowed a cat's yowl of displeasure, and everyone in the surrounding area swiveled toward the sound. The hound trotted in between a group of cowboys headed north and a buckboard headed south, a rather disgruntled calico held in his mouth as if he carried a stick, rather than the hissing, spitting creature. He leapt up to the porch, disregarding the blue streak the feline cussed or the yelp of concern from the kid as he dropped the creature gently to the boards. Shaking his head as if to clear it, the young man on the porch muttered something about the ill effects of drinking too much coffee before he stomped into the jailhouse, leaving us alone.

When the cat attempted to flee, the hound planted a rather large paw on her tail and flopped down on top of her. "Now, Miss Molly, we've need of your cleverness, and if you'd just come with me as I'd asked there'd be no need for such dramatics."

Though the calico growled, there was no real heat in it. After all, he'd appealed to her vanity. Call a cat clever or pretty, and they'd darn near defy the laws of nature to prove you right.

"There's no cause for this kind of dog-handling, Rufus," she complained, shrugging off one of his ears that had flopped over her flat face. "I'm a law-abiding citizen, and it's going to take ages to get the drool out of my coat."

"Indeed," Rufus replied with a calmness he shared with the soul who was clearly his master, lifting his massive frame off of her, though I noticed his paw remained in place. "But you'd have been ages about coming, and this is a time sensitive matter for the Sheriff."

"Fine." She sniffed, drawing herself up with the kind of imperiousness usually only seen in highly bred ladies, despite the drool matting her multicolored coat. "How may I be of service?"

I lowered my head to regard the cat, and blew gently, the otherworldly ether that kept me shiny washing over her. The cat's glowing green eyes widened with surprise as her fur smoothed and dried with no hint that she'd ever been touched.

"Well, I never! That's a handy trick, pretty horse. Do tell what I can offer to pay you back?"

"We need a telegram sent to Miller, Colorado, Miss Molly," I answered respectfully, ancient memories of the cats who'd lived in the stables of my youth coloring my address. "To one Brown, the ghost hunting dog. She's needed to deal with a possible haunting, once the outlaw being held is dispatched."

"A dog, you say?" Molly's eyes narrowed as she glared at Rufus.

"A dog?" Cole echoed, a hint of suspicion in his tone as well.

I drew my neck up high and looked down my nose at them both with a surety that comes with immortality. "Yes, along with her human, Elliott, she's gotten quite the reputation for hunting ghosts. I can assure you, she is definitely the dog for the job."

Cole sighed, wiping a hand over his face, and Molly sniffed imperiously.

"We've already plenty of dogs in this town, surely one of us could do the job," Rufus interjected, his head lifted with pride and a stubborn jut to his jaw.

"While I'm sure you could track a ghost to the ends of the earth, fine hound, Brown is a border collie. She has a knack for herding the ghosts into the traps her human sets, and holding them while they are dispelled."

"I've no wish for any more dogs, either, Rufus, but if this horse is sure she'll keep that ruffian from haunting our town, I'll do it." The bloodthirsty tone of the little house cat took me aback. "My mistress lost her husband to this bandit's evil, and I'd tear him apart like a mouse if I could, to repay her heartbreak. She'll be to bed soon, and I'll send the message then."

Then she stared imperiously at Rufus's paw until he lifted it away, and strolled down the boardwalk with a superior air until she was lost to sight.

"This's a lot to take in." Cole muttered, sitting on the edge of the porch beside Rufus. Absently, he reached to pet the dog, only to have his hand pass right through. Rufus shivered in reaction, but he leaned in closer anyway, clearly devoted to his human in any form. "Talking critters. All this time."

"Spirit comprehends far more than mind, Sheriff, and animals are much more in tune with spirit than man. The lack in mortal man often comes with ego, but that's all fallen away for you now."

"I dunno," Rufus directed a stubborn glare my way again. "Mr. Cole and I sure seemed to understand each other pretty well. So he's better than most humans."

Part of me wanted to scoff. Dogs were often blindly devoted to their humans. Yet, something about the fond look Cole slanted toward his hound kept my jaded opinion from rearing up in objection. Perhaps there was something better about this soul than the many others I'd met.

We passed the night peaceably enough after that, Cole content to resume his watch from the rocking chair. I settled into what passed for a doze, lazily switching my tail just for something to do as my head hung low. People went to bed, and the young deputy Cole called Evan yielded to the lure of sleep, his snoring the only steady sound throughout the night. When dawn came, I stretched my neck as high as I could, catching the first rays that aimed down the street.

A gasp of admiration from Cole made me turn my head, my neck curving at the perfect angle as the sun fully broke the horizon. My alabaster coat transformed, soft rainbows chasing their way through my mane and tail. I hadn't been able to admire the pinks and purples in my mortal days, but again, spirit saw what the mind could not. Now, while I wasn't exactly vain, I did understand the impressive figure I cut.

"Aube. No wonder. Now, that's a sight for sore eyes."

But the moment was broken by a ruckus inside the jail, and Cole shot out of his seat, straight through the wall. It amazed me how he could do that. Most spirits could not make use of physical constructs, like the porch or the chair, only able to hover above them. Yet, the strength of his convictions made it possible.

He did not reemerge until the town had come to life, shop keepers opening up shutters and children trudging along with books under their arms to attend school. A heavy sigh pulled my head around so I could study him, and I recognized a weight on his shoulders that I understood. Duty exhausted both body and spirit, and the urge to run away from it quivered under my skin. Recklessly, I sidled up beside the porch, arching my neck in excitement.

"Sheriff, care to chase the horizon with me?"

His brows shot up in surprise, but a smile broke free seconds afterward as he lightly vaulted onto my broad back. I barely waited for his hand to take a fistful of my mane before I launched down the street, nostrils stretched wide at the beckoning hint of freedom that came from a good gallop. We quickly found each other's rhythm, exploring canyons and arid plateaus at a speed that would have stolen mortal breath. But we were no more than specters, air barely more than a friction that lifted my mane and tail.

When full noon found us, I turned back to the town, Cole saying not a word until I had deposited him back at his station. Rufus waited, tail wagging and tongue lolling as his human dismounted. Though he leaned into Cole's ghostly leg, Cole petted him almost absently as he solemnly studied me.

"You know, Aube, I worried for a few that you might be taking me to my reward. But I'm grateful you didn't, though that ride was darn near heavenly on its own. Thank you."

I nodded my head thoughtfully, wondering when I'd last given myself over to that much unfettered joy. And to have found it with a human, of all things. "You are an honorable man, Cole. I could do no less."

Another night passed much as the first, though the next day brought a greater ruckus, as the judge arrived in town with the morning train. A hasty courtroom was constructed in the local dance hall, and people spilled into town to attend the afternoon trial. When the young deputy and a few other men gathered to escort the bandit, Cole joined them, and I caught my first glimpse of the man I'd learned had shot Cole in the back.

There was no remorse in the man's black eyes, and his sneer made my lips wrinkle with the same distaste I had for sage. I actually sneezed when he spat at the young deputy, wishing my incorporeal form could bite. Yet, Rufus had no such limits, and took a thick mouthful of the man's trouser leg to defend the boy. Both Cole and the boy called him off, though I heard pride in both their voices, and the hound sat beside me as they all disappeared through the swinging doors of the dance hall.

Cole reemerged a few minutes later, then sank into his rocker and tipped his hat down over his eyes. While the casual posture might have fooled a human, both Rufus and I shared a look, able to read the tension in his limbs, and the spicy scent of concern that muddied his spirit.

Still, a cheer went up hours later, and people spilled into the street to celebrate the conviction of the man who had plagued them for so long. A weight had lifted from all of them, smiles coming more easily, the sour stench of worry floating away on the breeze that cropped up around sunset. I felt Cole move up beside me, and my ears flicked toward him at the weight of his hand on my withers.

"Aube, you think I could trouble you for another gallop?"

Wordlessly, I bent a knee, allowing him to swing on. He settled easily, petting beneath my heavy mane as I paced more sedately down the street. But once we hit the outskirts of town, I lifted into a ground covering canter, carrying him away from his troubles, if only for a time.

The outlaw was set to hang the following day at sunset, and while there were restless mutterings through the night, the townsfolk waited. Their sheriff had been much beloved, and only his honorable example kept them from stringing the bandit up on their own. Gratefully, the morning brought another train, and with it, the welcome scent of a new dog once she cleared the smoky environs of the station.

The brown and white border collie trotted down the boardwalk with her tail eagerly lifted, a man in a round topped hat on her heels. Deputy Evan shot out of his chair as they approached, and the two men shook hands, while the dog went straight to greet Rufus.

"I'm Brown. I hear you have a ghost problem."

Rufus wagged his tail cautiously, then looked over at me. "This horse said we should call you."

Brown squinted her eyes at me and sneezed. "Think you could tone down the lights, horse?"

Though I pinned my ears slightly in irritation, I reeled in my spirit enough to make her more comfortable. "We don't have a ghost yet, but according to Cole, we'll have a vengeful spirit on our hands after tonight's hanging."

Cole nodded his confirmation, but then a verifiable curse from Evan pulled all of our attention. He collapsed into his chair, looking pale as the telegram fluttered from his fingers. I cocked my head to read it with one eye as it hit the porch, and Cole laughed.

"Well, seems Miss Molly signed the telegram with my name."

Understandably flustered, Evan took a few minutes to recover, and Brown went to her human. The man looked down at the border collie after Evan explained the situation. "What do you think, Brown? Do we have a ghost problem?"

She barked once, and lolled a doggie grin at him. Surprisingly, the man seemed to understand her, and got directions from the deputy to the nearest inn. Brown tossed a promise over her shoulder to return at sunset, lured away from our company by the offer of a steak. Rufus whined at the word, and thankfully, Deputy Evan had recovered enough to pick up on it.

"Come on, fella, let's go get you a steak, too. You've earned it."

He trotted off after the kid when Cole waved him away, and the sheriff smiled as they disappeared around the back side of the restaurant next door. I recognized a hint of weary resignation behind his expression of gladness. "I'm glad he'll have company after I've gone. Rufus is a good dog."

"You'll see him again," I assured the man, my own spine relaxing as Cole's posture lightened. "Dogs are devoted on either side of the veil."

He said nothing, but went back to his chair, lowering himself into the worn wooden slats with care. The day passed in a haze of dust as traffic moved about the town, and while I did not see Brown again, Rufus said he'd explained the situation to her. They'd be there when we needed them.

Sunset was masked a bit by the cloud cover, but Deputy Evan kept a close eye on his pocket watch, and at the appointed time, three men came to escort the bandit to his fate. He spewed hateful words at everyone he passed as they led him toward the edge of town, people falling in behind to be sure that justice was served. Cole didn't go with them this time, simply stood vigil, his hand tangled in my mane as if he might vault on so we could gallop away again. I shifted restlessly from hoof to hoof, nostrils flaring in anticipation of the coming fight. Mortal memories snuck through, flashes of battle making my neck arch, my tail flag.

The fading light dimmed even more, and I knew the time had come. Trumpeting a battle cry, I barely noticed as Cole swung aboard, and I reared as a chill wind pushed harshly down the street.

"Sheriff!" an otherworldly voice screamed, and I lashed out at the cold shade that darted toward me. It spun away on a cackle of mad laughter, shooting through the open window of a nearby building to wink out all the lights, and screams followed in its wake.

Out the corner of my eye, I saw Brown dart into the street, her human hot on her heels. He squinted his eyes against the dust being stirred up by the vengeful spirit, but when Brown picked up a stick and began to inscribe a circle in the dirt, he immediately jumped on the idea. When the wraith appeared a block away, and headed straight for us, I understood how I could help.

"Hold on!" I hollered, and Cole's legs gripped my barrel as I tore away from the center of town. We led the phantasm on a merry chase, and I toyed with him, darting between buildings and around objects. Cole laughed when the spirit couldn't corner and tumbled through the side of the church with hair-raising moan of frustration. While I had centuries to master my spirit form, this evil man had only known his for mere moments, and I would use it to our advantage several more times before Brown's bark of excitement brought us back toward the crossroads of the town.

We flew around the corner of the general store, and I aimed for the circle drawn on the ground, rocking back on my hocks to slide to a stop before we reached it. After all, I didn't want Cole or myself to get caught in the trap. But the ghost proved canny enough to swing around us, swiping at my passenger with gaunt fingers, tattering the fabric of Cole's spirit on the way by. Wheeling around to keep my eyes on the wily outlaw, I bared my teeth in threat, and Brown barked to get my attention.

"Can you slow him down enough that I can catch him?" She called out, and I nodded briefly before cantering forward.

Cole seemed to catch the spirit of the thing, and I threw my head back as he pulled open his coat, the shine from his badge adding to our already stinging glow. "Come on out and fight, you lily livered varmint! You want me? Well, you can't shoot me in the back this time!"

A watery giggle erupted as the spirit manifested between us and the trap, and I kept my eyes on it as I paced forward. I couldn't give Cole a verbal warning without giving away my plan, but when I rocked my weight back on my haunches, I felt his hand tighten in my mane.

"What are you going to do, Sheriff? You couldn't stop me in life, and you sure in tarnation can't do a thing to me in death! Now, I'm free!"

As the howling words lifted the hair on my withers, I spun around and lashed out with a hind foot as I had learned in my years as a warhorse. The howl gurgled to a wet halt as the specter flew backward, landing inches from the edge of the trap. It scrabbled to escape, but Brown moved in, low to the ground, her gaze freezing it in place. Inch by inch, she crept forward, forcing it into the circle, and a flare of light bright as the noonday sun made me flinch as the specter was caught.

Brown's human finished an incantation as the phantasm raged against its new jail, and as Elliott threw salt on the apparition, it vanished in a wet pop. All of us froze as ghostly slime coated our bodies, but then a baying cry broke the sudden silence as Rufus rounded the end of the street with Deputy Evan on his heels. I shook my head to dislodge the worst of the wet from my ears, and snorted loudly to eject the stench of ghost from my nostrils. The musty ozone smelled even worse than sage.

The human petted Brown's ears, and he laughed as his hand slid through the slime. "Well, Brown, I think we're due for another salt water bath."

Brown's ears flattened in distaste as Rufus skidded to a stop just outside the wide circle of slime, and I paced forward as the more natural light of dusk returned to the sky. I watched the human's eyes widen as the light caught on the film that coated us, making me momentarily visible to the mortal, but when I blew out an ether filled breath to cleanse them, he smiled graciously and tipped his hat in thanks.

But then Deputy Evan demanded an explanation from Elliott, and I stepped back, pushing spirit outward hard enough to dislodge the remaining ick on my coat. Cole dismounted, pulling off his cowboy hat to try and shake the sticky liquid off, but I breathed over him too. Without his hat on, I noticed he had blue eyes pale enough to rival my own.

"My thanks, Aube. Mighty kind of you. Do we have time for me to say my goodbyes?"

I nodded once, my ears pricked forward with amusement. "Of course, Cole. After all, it's not long in the greater scheme of eternity."

He laughed and took a few steps away, whistling to call Rufus to him. The rangy hound galloped over and went belly up like a puppy, whining against the farewell he knew was coming.

"Now, now, my good fellow, you've a job to do, keeping Evan safe. And Aube says we'll see each other again." The hound cast me a mournful eye, and I nodded vigorously, which set the dog's thick tail wagging again. "You know where my star is, don't you, my boy?"

Rufus leapt to his feet, long tongue lolling from his floppy jowls. "Yes, Mr. Cole, I sure do!"

"Then you find it and give it to Evan for me, okay? I know this town will be safe if I leave it to the two of you." Then he patted the hound's head, and Rufus pushed into the contact, even as the chill of the otherworld made him shiver. "You've been the best dog, Rufus."

Rufus wrinkled his lips. "No sir, we had to call in for help from that Brown dog!"

Cole chuckled. "Rufus, she was the best dog for the job. A good sheriff knowns when he needs help, just like you knew we needed help from Miss Molly. But I know you're the best dog for this town, and this boy."

"Yes, Mr. Cole, I sure am!" He answered, and when Cole straightened, the black and brown hound took up his post, circling around to lean against Deputy Evan's leg. Evan crouched down to stroke Rufus's ears, all wide-eyed amazement as Elliott explained an animal's natural connection to the otherworldly, telling tales of the many ghosts Brown had helped him with.

Cole jammed his hat back on his head and turned toward me with a smile. "Hey Aube, we got time for one last ride before you deliver me?"

I bent my knee in answer, and this time when he climbed aboard, it was me that sighed. I'd miss this easy companionship. Horses weren't mean to be alone, mortal or not. We galloped up to the top of the nearest plateau, just catching the last winking light of sunset it my mane before it disappeared. The clouds cleared as we moved through the desert, stars peppering the darkness and the moon bright enough to shine against my ethereal hide.

A deep breath of the night air from my passenger brought me to a halt on the edge of a canyon, and I gave him a moment to come to terms with his fate. But when he spoke, the words surprised me.

"Aube, I thought you said spirit couldn't fight ghosts. But you sure packed a punch against that spook. How is that?"

Honorable, brave and clever. Cole McInnis's unexpected partnership continued to delight, and I arched my neck in justifiable pride over the privilege of carrying him. "I am different. I chose this in between, not quite of one world or another, and able to interact with both, if I want. I can even choose to be seen, if I have need. We are all given a choice on the other side."

Silence reigned as a shower of meteors painted the night, but when the last flare had passed, Cole spoke again. "Well then, Aube, I wonder if I can choose to stay with you? I think we'd make a fine team, bringing in those who seek to evade judgment. Do you think that's possible?"

My ears pricked forward, skin quivering at the prospect. But Cole's hand stroked over my neck, immediately soothing the nervous excitement. "I don't know, Cole, but I'd like to find out. We'll have to pass through the veil to discover the answer. Are you ready?"

His hand tightened in my mane, the only sign of nervousness he would allow, and I felt a smile lighten his body. "I'm ready for my reward, Aube."

I reared up in excitement, throwing us into the air over the canyon, Cole giving a "Yeehaw!" as my hooves found purchase in the thin fabric of the world. As we galloped through the veil, moving as one, I hoped we would both find our reward on the other side.

The End

When she isn't writing, J.D. is most often found amongst the horses. Either in the barn or the field, they draw her away from her desk and refill the well that her stories come from. It the call of spirit, the sort that dwells deep within every living thing, and lingers even after the flesh is gone. Or at least that's how she feels, which is what prompted this story. All of J.D.'s stories feature animals as characters, whatever shape they may take, and the important role they have in human lives (and after lives). If you have ever been touched by one of the animals in your own life, then you understand. You can find more on J.D., her animals, and her stories, on Facebook, at
https://www.facebook.com/AuthorJDHarrison/

KITTY AND PITTY SAVE THE NEIGHBORHOOD

BY SHOSHANAH HOLL

It was a good day to be a dog because it was a good day to run around the yard. I did a little dance at the back door before my human let me out.

"Bosco, sit." I whimpered a little, but sat down as well as I could while wagging my tail. Sometimes you can't control the tail. Especially when you knew those squirrels were out in the yard. Those jerks! All over my yard! Didn't even know what was going to hit them. This time, for sure...my human waited a minute, and then he cracked the door and I was out.

The squirrels scattered back up into the tree, of course. Always too fast no matter how I ran. But I hopped up on my hind legs against the trunk anyway.

"Hey! Hey! You stay out of my yard!"

A big gray jerk with a huge bushy tail scowled at me, just barely out of reach. If only I was good at jumping. He chittered something insulting at me then

117

scuttled back up the tree. I barked after him. "Yeah! You better run!"

"Boss, chill out. You're not gonna get them." My human sounded more amused than angry.

I sighed, but dropped back down. My human was right, of course; he always was. I wished I was as smart as my human. He's the smartest animal I ever met.

He stood on the back deck puffing smoke while I patrolled the yard. It was cold, but not so cold that he put sweaters on me. I liked being warm, but the humans always took so many pictures when I wore sweaters that I had to think it seemed...cute. Undignified. What's a dog without his dignity? A pup, that's what. But it was cold enough that there were leaves piling over the grass. Humans had started cutting up pumpkins and putting them out. I don't know why they did that, but since I wasn't allowed to chew on the pumpkins it probably didn't matter. I snuffled through a pile of extra-crunchy leaves, catching whiffs of rabbit and maple and squirrel and something else, something rotten and unpleasant...

"Hey, loser."

I jumped out of the pile, shedding leaves everywhere. A black cat with a bright red collar strolled along the top of the fence, watching me. "Cat friend! Cat! Hello!" I jumped up at the fence, and looked back to my human. "Look! The cat is here!"

He glanced up from his phone. "Boss, leave the kitty alone."

118

The cat glared at me. Or maybe that's just what he always looked like. It's hard to tell, with cats.

"Are you done yet?"

I sat down. "I'm so happy to see you, cat friend!"

Boo hopped down from his fence and eyed me. "Wish I could say the same, but I could smell you a mile away. Doesn't your human give you baths?"

I hung my head. "I just had one." I respected my human's wisdom, but I didn't understand why he wanted me to smell like soap and water. I always tried to share my best smells with him, in his bed or on his couch but he just said, "Oh god, what *is* that?" or "Why does it smell like a fish's butthole in here?" There were some things about my human I'd never understand.

Boo rubbed against my leg. No doubt trying to make me stink like cat. Ugh. "If you say so." He squinted out at the alley. "Been a little quiet around here, hasn't it?"

I cocked my head. It wasn't quiet at all; there were little humans running and screaming on the street and cars driving. "It has?"

The cat huffed at me. "Not literally, you dolt. I mean for us. Not many pets out. I only got barked at once today on my rounds."

I frowned at that. He was right; I hadn't seen half the dogs I used to stop and share sniffs with when we went on a walk yesterday, and barely any cats.

"Weird."

"Weird times in the neighborhood, my friend." He suddenly went rigid, tail puffed up. "Do you smell that?"

119

I lifted my nose to the wind. Old diapers, rabbit poop, squirrels, dead squirrel, the pizza in the dumpster my human wouldn't share...then something awful. Really nasty. Worse than bad pizza nasty. That bad rotten thing I'd smelled earlier, but with burning in it too.

"Trashcan?" I tried.

Cat stared at me, then climbed to his feet and walked away. "I swear to the Nine Lives, I don't know why I even try."

I cast one last look at the alley, but the awful smell made me nervous. I followed Boo.

"Well, what's your point?"

"My point is that no one's taking their pets out, and there's bad things on the wind. Something's afoot."

I looked down at my feet. Everything about my paws seemed normal.

"Boo! Mister Boo-berry!"

The cat froze, ears pricked up. I recognized his human's voice from the alleyway. The latch on the gate clattered and I bolted for it. Just in case it was some kind of intruder's trick, you know, faking a familiar voice. But it was just the human from next door. Boo's human was smaller than mine, which made sense since the cat was smaller than me, but she was strong and ready for my jumps.

"Oof! Hey, Boss." She laughed and caught my collar with one hand. "Easy, buddy. Sit!"

I plopped down, but kept wagging for her. Anyone who took care of my cat friend was a good human and deserved wags. She grinned and held out her hand.

"Can I have a shake?"

Could she! I was so ready to shake! I tried to give her both paws, but then I fell over. So I settled for just one. She shook it, laughed again, and stood up.

Boo came strolling over to her, eyes big and watery with adoration.

"Mama." He rubbed against her ankles and wound around her legs, purring. "Mama. Hi, mama. Love you, mama."

I never had the heart to tell him his mother probably wasn't a human. In my limited experience, human pups were hairless, sticky, and prone to grabbing things Especially ears. And tails. Definitely not kittens, which were mostly fluffy, curious, and very sharp. But if he believed she was his mother and it made him happy, I wasn't going to tell him. That would just be mean. Not at all what a Good Boy would do.

She rubbed his ears. "There's my handsome boy." My human waved from the porch. "Hey, Lisa. How's it going?"

She waved back. "Fine, fine. Just looking for this little miscreant." She scooped Boo up with one arm and he grumbled at her.

"Mother, I am more than old enough to get home by myself..." But then she started rubbing his chin and he trailed off into a purr. My human hopped off the porch and caught me by the collar.

"Sorry about him jumping."

"Oh, Boss is fine." She scratched my ear with one free hand. "He's a big old baby."

I was not. I was a big, strong dog. But she was very good at ear scratches, so I let it slide. Might have drooled a little.

My human chuckled. "He really is. I just know most people see a pit bull running at them and freak out."

She snorted. "I've never met a bad dog. Dogs with bad owners, maybe. Besides," she lifted Boo, curled in the crook of her arm, "I know all about owning a scary pet."

My human held his fingers out for Boo. The cat sniffed them delicately, then headbutted his hand. "He's a real terror."

She grinned, and kissed the cat on his forehead. Boo wrinkled his nose and made a great show of distaste, but never stopped purring.

"Did he escape?" My human rubbed Boo's chin. I was not jealous. Not at all. I just lifted my chin a bit so he would remember that he could give me scratches too.

"Little terror. I've been keeping him in with all the people losing their animals, but he always seems to find a way out." She rubbed Boo's stomach. He stretched out to give her access.
"Mama. Best belly rubs, Mama. The best."

It was sort of sad to see a creature of his dignity reduced to that state, I thought...while still drooling a little from ear scratches. My human shook his head.

"That's messed up. I hope they figure out what's going on soon. You know Marni, that annoying little dachshund down the way?"

I certainly did. Any dog so small and so angry tended to make an impression. The cat lady nodded.

My human shook his head. "Gone. A couple nights ago. Just vanished."

She suddenly smelled frightened, and hugged Boo close.

"Poor pup. I'm always careful with him, you know, around Halloween, but this year...it's just awful."

My human nodded and gave me a one-arm hug. It took years for me to understand hugs are good; humans are weird like that. Squeezing another animal is how they show they love it. No, I do not understand. Like many things about my human, I just accept it. Like a Good Boy.

Whenever somebody knocked on the door, I made sure to let my human know. Several times, in case he didn't catch it the first.

"Intruder! Intruder!" I barreled down the hall and he ran from the kitchen.

"Damnit, Bosco, stay put!"

"INTRUDER!" I jumped up against the door as the intruder knocked again. No matter what awful beasts might be out there, I was ready. Until my human caught me by the collar and pulled me back down, anyway.

"Sit! Behave yourself!"

I sat down, but could not promise behaving under the threat of intruders. He squinted at the peephole, then opened the door. I wanted to go sniff, but his hand was still on my collar, so I was a Good Boy and sat. I didn't recognize the two humans at the door, but I'd definitely smelled them around the neighborhood. They were older than mine, and even when one of them smiled they didn't look happy to see either of us. Worse, they smelled scared and angry. And like chicken.

"Mister Brenner. Glad we finally caught you."

My human eyed them suspiciously. "Can I help you?"

"Oh, I'm so sorry. We're with the neighborhood association." She smiled another one of those big, bright smiles that looked mean and held out her hand. My human looked at her hand like it was a slobbery chew toy, but shook it anyway. He wouldn't even touch my toys when I brought them to him all nice and chewed up, but he'd shake a mean human's hand? Unbelievable. "I'm Beverly, and this is Nick. We live down the block."

"Nice to meet you. How can I help you?"

"Well, I'm sure you've heard about some people's pets going missing." She looked at me. It was not a nice look, like I was a dirty, smelly Bad Dog. I pressed a little closer to my human. "We're going around talking to people, you know, in case anyone's seen anything."

"Oh, right. I heard about that." My human shook his head. "It's awful. I haven't seen anything though."

"Any strange noises? Suspicious people?"

"Nothing. Sorry."

"Do you keep him on a leash?" The male human hadn't talked yet, and his voice was as mean as the look he was giving me. My human's hand tightened on my collar.

"Boss? Not in the yard when I let him out, but yeah, if we're on a walk."

"And you're always out there with him? Always?" Humans aren't very good at growling, but my human might as well have. "What are you implying?"

The stranger shrugged. "Most of the animals going missing are smaller. Corgis, cats. If there's a big, aggressive dog going unattended..."

"Bosco isn't aggressive. And he doesn't go around attacking other animals." My human said firmly. I wagged my tail once. The stranger snorted.

"Yeah, sure, pit bull that's not aggressive." The woman elbowed him.

"Well, if you're sure you haven't seen anything..."

"I *am*." My human went to close the door. "Thanks for stopping by."

The woman's smile finally faded a bit. "Welcome to the neighborhood. Hopefully you'll remember us well when you leave in March."

My human frowned. "Why would I leave in March?"

"The district's ban on aggressive breeds goes into effect." She eyed me and I ducked my head behind my human. "Trying to keep our neighborhood a little safer, you know."

My human didn't slam the door, but he shut it hard enough to make me jump.

125

"Aggressive breeds! You gotta be *kidding* me."

He stormed back into the kitchen, and after a backward look at the door where the awful humans had been, I followed him. He was sitting on the floor next to the big cold food box, glaring at his phone. He looked angry, but I could smell how scared and upset he was. I whined a little. Why would other humans want to make him sad? He was definitely a Good Boy. The very best. Whatever was on his phone must have been bad because he put it down and ran a hand through his hair.

I sat next to him and whined again. He sighed.

"It's okay, Boss." He hugged me close to him. "If we have to move, I'll...figure something out. I won't give you up." Of course he would figure things out. That's what humans did. They always found a way to make things okay. So I stood patiently while he squeezed me too hard, buried his face in my fur and started crying a little.

Because I was a Good Boy.

The next day when he let me out, I did my business quick (with only one little woof up at the stupid squirrels) and jumped up against the fence.

"Cat! Cat friend!"

Sharp claws sounded loud on their way up the fence, then black head poked up to scowl down at me.

"Moron. What do you want?"

I dropped down to my haunches. "I need help." The cat eyed me a moment, then scrambled awkwardly up onto the top of the fence.

"What on earth for?"

I hung my head. "My human is in trouble."

Cat friend tilted his head, looking confused. "What's wrong with him?"

I hung my head. "Other humans. They want him to go away because of me."

The cat paused in the middle of licking his tail. "What's wrong with you?"

My ears drooped almost as low as I felt. "They think I'm a Bad Dog. That I hurt other pets."

"What nonsense." The cat hopped off the fence and slunk around me. "Don't you listen to them."

I whined a little, still hanging my head. I wanted nothing more than to just be a Good Boy; it wasn't my fault I was big and something bad happened to those other pets. The cat looked at me and flicked his tail.

"Look, some humans are just mean and dumb. Stupid as a squirrel. There's no way around it. Did you know someone kicked me the other day, when I was out for a stroll?"

"A human?"

"Yes! I just went up to introduce myself, see if, you know, maybe he had any interest in some chin scratches or something, and he kicked me! Said he didn't want any bad luck." Cat friend's ears flattened and the fur on his back rose up at the memory. "Only bad luck I give is a clawed-up face, if someone ever tries to *kick* me again."

127

I was pretty sure that counted as not Good Boy behavior, but cats had their own ideas of how to be a Good Boy. Being a Bad Cat seemed to involve more climbing on things and hairballs than Bad Dog. The chewing was pretty much the same, though.

The cat shook himself a little, and settled down in front of me. "So, what do you want to do about it?"

I snuffed at a patch of dirt, catching an old whiff of rabbit. "Dunno. But people need to know I'm a good boy, and I wouldn't hurt any other pets."

Cat friend chewed on a bit of grass thoughtfully. "Well. It seems to me the simplest thing is to find out what *is* hurting those other pets."

I cocked my head at that. "You mean go find them."

He coughed a little, then swallowed the last bit of grass. "Makes sense, don't you think?"

"But..." I looked up at the gate to the back alley. "But that's *outside*."

"Don't be a ninny. I go outside all the time and I'm just fine."

"But you're a cat!" As far as I could tell, there was no way to keep a cat inside if they didn't want to be there. Believe me, the humans sure tried.

"And you're a big, strong dog. What do you have to be scared of?"

I nosed at the ground. "I guess..."

The cat stood and twitched his tail disdainfully. "I'll go on reconnaissance."

"On what?"

He huffed. "Scouting. I'll catch you out here later, all right?"

I was one lucky dog—my human called me back before I had to answer. I took off for the back door like a streak.

"You better be here, you big coward!"

I ducked behind my human and tried to pretend I hadn't heard him.

I'm a simple dog with simple tastes. A nice evening in. My human had a book, I had a rawhide, so maybe I forgot about the whole thing. Just a little bit. Or a lot a bit. When my human let me out one last time before bed, I trotted right out without a second thought. The whole yard stank of rabbit, and I peeked behind some of the bushes hopefully. I didn't even notice Cat friend until he came streaking into the yard, shrieking.

I hopped out of the bush, on high alert, and tripped over my feet.

"Cat? Cat!"

"Bad! Bad, bad, bad!" He bolted straight up onto the porch and was hiding behind my human's legs before he even saw him. My human said a bad word, dancing away.

"Jesus, Boo! You scared the crap out of me." Cat stood his ground, pressed close against my human with all his fur on end.

"Bad stuff, Dog! Real bad!"

My human frowned, kneeling down to scratch the cat's ears. I was not jealous at all. Honest.

"Boo-Berry? What's wrong?" The cat accepted the petting, but stayed arched up, growling at the alleyway he'd come from. I took a wary step toward the gate.

"Boss, you stay put."

I stopped, but stayed on high alert. The breeze changed a little, and I got a whiff of something bad from the alley. Worse than that old pizza in the trashcans, which was pretty bad. My human leaned against the gate, squinting out into the dark alley.

"What's up, Boo? A raccoon get you?"

Cat shot him a dirty look from the porch. "You think some dumb *raccoon* could do this?"

My human ignored his yowl and opened the gate. I knew he wouldn't want me to, but this was time to be brave so I shoved past him and ran out into the alley.

"Bosco! Damnit, Boss, you get back here!"

I snuffled down the way Cat had come from. It was bad, alright. Blood and burning stuff, and something nasty and rotten. My human came running after me, but I beat him around the dumpster and found the dog first.

I didn't know him, but all the black labs I've known were good boys and he had a collar on so he must have had a human. But there was no human here, just a dying dog. I stopped short and my human ran into me.

"Bosco, what the he..." He stopped. "Oh, my god."

I whined. Something had ripped that Good Boy up and left him here. There was so much blood and claw marks on him, I only knew he was a lab from the scent. He whimpered and lifted his head a little. I took a slow step forward. He smelled like the bad thing I'd caught a whiff of in the yard a few days ago; burning hair and old, spoiled meat. But all of his wounds were too fresh to be rotten. My human grabbed me by the collar.

"Inside! Now!"

I hung my head but let him lead me back to our yard and in the back door, though I kept looking back at that poor dog. He scooped Cat up with one hand and tossed him after me. Cat friend landed with a yowl of outrage.

"You too, buddy. Lisa would kill me if anything happened to you."

He slammed the door shut and went hurrying back to the alley with his phone out. Cat friend and I looked at each other, then back out the window. More humans showed up, and finally we heard the sound of a little human crying. I hopped down from the window with a huff. Cat's whiskers drooped.

"Do you think that's what happened to the other pets?" I said. Cat never looked away from the window, but his tail twitched.

"I don't know." He looked down at me. "But we have to find them to make sure."

I hung my head, but he was right. I didn't want any other Good Boys to end up like that. Or any more little humans crying over them.

We went on our mission the next evening. My human was gone, but Cat and I had long ago figured out how to get the screen door open. It felt wrong, going out with no human, and I hung my head low. Cat glanced back at me with a huff.

"Are you coming or what?"

"I'm coming!" I glanced back at the porch. My human would be so upset if we weren't back before him. This was Bad Dog territory, no doubt about it. But...it would be really Bad Dog to let anything happen to the other animals, too. I sighed. This was why I let my human figure things out. I headbutted the gate to get it open and followed Cat friend out into the alley.

"Where are we going?"

He had perched on a trash can, scenting the air and tail whipping.

"Your magical nose will help with that."

I eyed him. "This is just my regular nose."

The cat huffed. "You're the one always bragging about how well you can smell *anything*. That dog last night stank; we follow his trail, we find where he got attacked."

It made sense, but I didn't like it. I didn't like any of this.

The cat hopped down from the trash can.

"Let's go."

I whined a little. "This seems like a bad idea."

"What are you, chicken?"

Well, that was silly. Chickens were delicious. Unless they were alive. Then they were very mean.

"No, I'm a dog."

The cat huffed. "It'll be fine. We're being brave. It's rock and roll."

I cocked my head. "Why would you roll a rock?"

He wrinkled his nose. "It's just something my human says."

"What does it mean?" All I could picture was a field of big boulders, rolling along all by themselves. Scary stuff.

"No idea. She usually says it before or after she does something stupid."

"You're not making me feel better."

"I know."

Cat friend was right. It *stank* where that poor dog had been. A pup could have followed that trail. I snuffed back and forth for across the alley while he stood watch. There were an awful lot of humans out for it being after dark, even the little ones. Even with all their noise and the bad smells of oil and trash and, ugh, raccoons in the alley, the scent was easy to pick up. I finally stopped at the end of the alley.

"This way."

Cat friend squinted out at the sidewalk.

"You sure?"

"Of course I'm sure." Mostly.

We set off down the sidewalk, trying hard to look innocent. Nothing wrong with a dog and a cat out for a walk. Fortunately, most of the humans out weren't paying any attention to us. They were all out in confusing costumes, going from door to door with a lot of shrieking and laughing. Almost every door had one of those cut-up pumpkins at it, and I gave one a sad look as we went by. They just looked like they'd be so *fun* to chew on...

"You better be paying attention." Cat muttered as we passed a bunch of young humans throwing toilet paper up in a tree. Cat's eyes gleamed.

"What a waste. Didn't even shred it a little..." He shook his head. "Anyway. We still on the trail?"

"I think so." I sniffed at a fire hydrant as we passed. A whole lot of dogs smelled on it, and if I thought cat friend would let me stop, I'd have added my own mark to it. But the bad smell was getting stronger as we walked. Still all that spoiled meat and burnt hair.

It was a stinky trail through the neighborhood, leading us right up to one of the streets my human always skipped on our walks. There weren't so many people here, and hardly any of the houses had lights on. Most of them were old and looked sad, with broken windows or boards over the door. Even the sidewalk was cracked and sprouting weeds. Cat looked around warily.

"You sure this is right?"

"Smell for yourself." Because the smell was awful now. Really bad. No way even a human couldn't have noticed. He flattened his ears a little.

"We must be close."

The narrow road went around to a dead end, and even if I hadn't been able to smell it, I'd have known that was the right place. It was big and broken down, but with flickering lights in the windows and the door standing open like a hungry mouth. Even squirrels were nowhere to be found near that thing. I nosed around the foot of the stairs leading up to it. No way to miss it. This was the place.

Cat arched his back, tail fluffing up. "Charming."

I whined a little before I realized what I was doing, and tried to look brave. It was really hard. My tail stayed right between my legs. Always had a mind of its own. Right now, I agreed with it. Cat started up the steps, and I followed two or three behind.

"Maybe we should just go home, Cat friend..." As we got closer to the house, my ears pricked at the sound of voices inside. "Leave this for the humans to deal with."

"Are you a whimpering puppy or a grown dog?" The cat hissed back at me. I realized I *was* whimpering a little, under my breath, and stopped. But it was hard because I really just wanted to go home and sleep on the bed until my human got back.

But instead we went up through the front door. I could smell other animals, now—the dog from the night before was strong, but other dogs and cats too. But there were human smells too, with all that nasty burning, and I hung back at the door.

"There's humans in there."

"So?" Cat looked back at me, eyes gleaming.

"So what are we supposed to do about humans?"

"You're seventy pounds of killing machine. Act like it."

I didn't want to act like any kind of machine, let alone a killing one. I whined loudly.

"Cat!"

"What?"

"I want to go home!"

"For the love of Bast, we've come all this way! Don't you want to know what's going on?"
"I don't care." It was true, too. Curiosity might have killed the cat. But dogs? We were just fine.

Cat flicked his tail disdainfully. "Fine. Be that way. Go crying home to your human. I'll take care of it myself." He trotted into the house, hair fluffed up to make him look twice as big and tail sticking out. I waited a minute in case he changed his mind, but he was gone. I sighed and turned back out the door, taking the stairs two at a time. I would run home as fast as I could and hope my human wouldn't be too mad that I had gotten out. He might yell at me, but surely he'd still let me share the bed tonight.

I almost made it off the creepy street when I heard Cat friend shriek. Not meow or howl, but screaming just like he had in the alley last night. I froze. The scream rose up loud, and then stopped dead. I lifted my nose to the wind; nothing but that bad, awful smell. I couldn't go back. But I couldn't leave Cat behind. He was trying his best to be a Good Boy in a cat way. And his human would be so sad.

"Cat?" I called. No reply. "Cat friend!" Nothing. But I heard a human laugh inside, and it was *mean* laugh. Like something rabid. My hackles rose hearing it. I was so scared I shook, but...I had to be a Good Boy. Would a Good Dog leave his friend behind?

I knew the answer to that.

I bolted up the stairs. A human was closing the door, but I hit it at a full run and knocked it wide open, sending him to the ground. He smelled bad, not just that burning smell but like he didn't wash. I hoped I wouldn't have to bite him because there was no way it would taste good. He yelped as he fell, and I walked toward him, stiff-legged and growling.

"Holy crap!"

"What is it *now*, Andre?"

"Dog! Big ass dog!"

Someone came from the other room and stopped in the door way.

"Is that damn pit bull?"

I growled louder. The man lying on the ground whimpered. The other one just looked angry.

"Get in here already! It's almost midnight and I've got the ritual set up! We'll just lock it out."

The human crawled toward his friend and before I could follow, they slammed a door in my face. I threw myself against it, but it didn't give even a little bit. I sat back and glared at the knob. Hands! If I even just had a thumb, all the things I could do...but no good chewing that old bone. Had to be another way in. I snuffed around the house, but it was hard to catch anything with that awful burned smell. I wandered into a kitchen full of rotten human food, trailing the smell of smoke to a vent. It was a big hole, but I was a big dog, and I had to squish myself down to fit in. Worse, it was full of mouse poop. And spiderwebs. And a few living spiders.

"Don't go. Danger! Bad things!" They whispered to me as I passed by. I'd never known that spiders could be scared of anything.

"Gotta go. Friend needs me."

They whispered to themselves, but stayed back and let me by. I wiggled through to a covered vent and peeked out at the awful humans. They had a room full of candles and a big dark circle on the floor that smelled like, ugh, dog blood. But the worst was a squirming, hissing bag in the middle of the circle.

"...kill you, claw your faces right off, every worthless mother's son of you, just let me out and I swear by the Nine Lives I'll take you all with one paw tied behind my back..." Cat was being brave, but even I could see there was no way out of the bag. I whined a little, but neither of the humans seemed to notice, staring down at an old book.

"You sure we got this right, man?"

"Of course I'm sure. You're not going to back out now, are you?"

The smaller human shook his head. "No, no, I just want to be sure we got it right. The book says, you know, with summoning...if you mess up even the smallest thing..."

The other man slapped the book shut. "I haven't been snatching animals for the past three months just to goof it up now, okay? This is perfect. We have the circle, the house where a murder took place, and now the black cat. Three minutes to midnight on Halloween, and when we call this thing up, we get anything we want. Money. Girls. *Magic.* You name it."

The smaller man nodded, but I could smell how scared he was. Good. I headbutted the grate over the vent, and it scooted forward a little. I wiggled forward and hit it harder. It slipped out of place with a scrape, and one of the humans looked up.

"Did you hear something?"

His friend scowled. "I hear an idiot who's about to get an ass-kicking if you don't let me read. This Latin is super weird."

I held my breath and nudged at the grate. If I could just go slow...but then the tall one took out a big, shiny knife and I knew the time to be careful was gone.

"Alright. Let's have a look at mister kitty." He reached one hand for the bag full of Cat Friend.

The time had come to be a Brave Boy.

I burst out of the vent and rammed straight into the shorter human. He didn't even have time to scream as I jumped on him and growled straight into his face.

"BAD HUMAN!"

He went pale and froze. His friend was so shocked he didn't even notice one black paw poke out of the bag he'd started to untie, until Cat swiped him across the hand. The human with the knife was bad, but I winced; I'd gotten clawed up by an angry cat before.

The human dropped the bag and Cat friend wriggled free.

"Dead. Dead. All of you, dead!"

"Cat!"

He looked back at me, tail twitching. He seemed surprised.

"You came back?"

"Of course! I'm a Good Boy!" The man I was standing on whimpered a little.

The one with the knife glared at me. "What the hell is this?"

He really shouldn't have said anything. Cat was still on full alert and spat at him, slashing at his ankles.

He backed away, tripping over one of the candles and fell, slicing his arm open. The blood landed inside the circle and hissed like hot oil. Cat darted away to stand by me, eyes wide.

"What was that? And what's that smell?"

He was right. It smelled awful. Worse than the time my human singed his hair on the grill. The wooden floor suddenly cracked where the blood had fallen and I jumped off the human to run away. Cat and I backed up against the wall, but the humans just sat there watching. And they say *we're* the dumb ones.

"What's happening?" I howled.

"How should I know?" Cat spat back. "Nothing good!"

The floor crumbled away like an old dog biscuit and fire light shone through. From the hole I heard screaming, like a whole crowd of humans hurting. The human I'd knocked down crawled backward, but the one Cat had gotten lay in the circle groaning. The whole house shook and rumbled. Cat's ears were flat against his head, and my tail firmly between my legs.

The rumbling stopped, but light still shone under the floor as the human in the circle stood up and shook his head. When he looked up, his eyes glowed with the same light. The whole room stank like burning and rotten meat.

"Uh oh." I said very, very softly. Cat glared at me.

"Yes, moron. Uh oh."

The human laying on the floor whimpered, and I suddenly smelled human pee. Why would he think now was a good time to mark his territory?

140

The glowing human took a step towards us, looking down at his hands like he'd never seen them.

"Flesh. Form. Yes." He rubbed his hands together. "At last. At long last."

The other human cleared his throat. "Are...are you okay, man?"

His friend's head snapped up like a cat spotting a mouse.

"You. You idiots. Did you think you could keep me enslaved? Try to sustain me with the blood of lesser beasts?" He pointed at us and I whimpered. Cat's tail twitched; he just looked mad about being called a lesser beast.

The other human's mouth was open. "I didn't mean...we didn't..." He waved at the book on the floor. "Gary translated it, man! I don't know any Latin! He said it was okay!"

His friend smiled, and showed a big, big mouth full of teeth too sharp for any human. Or any dog.

"I'm going to enjoy devouring your soul first. Such as it is."

The other human whimpered and tried to crawl to the door. As the glowing human stepped forward, I growled. He looked at us, shining eyes narrowed.

"I've no quarrel with you, little ones. Don't make one."

His mouth moved like a human talking, but when he said it I heard him growl it liked a dog and hiss it like a cat at the same time. The fur on my neck stood up. Cat didn't wait for him to say anything else.

I've seen a lot of brave things, but I don't think many of them were dumber than Cat friend launching

141

himself straight onto the bad human's face. The human didn't expect it either and stumbled back, screaming so high and awful it hurt my ears. But Cat was out for blood, all claws and teeth and the bad human couldn't shake him off as he stumbled back.

"His...legs...moron!" Cat hissed. I shook myself and dove forward. I am not skilled at many things, but I've always been good at getting humans all tangled up; they only have two legs, so you'd think they would be better at using them.

The bad human was no exception. He tripped over me and toppled backwards, down through the hole in the floor, into the fire. His shriek faded away as he fell and fell for a long time. Cat barely managed to get a claw hooked on the edge of floor.

"Friend!"

"I got it! Leave me be!" He was clearly slipping back.

"Let me help you!"

"I don't need any help!" He was losing his grip. I dipped my head towards him.

"So help me Bast, if you get that slobbery mouth anywhere near me..." But I already had caught him in my mouth and dumped him on the floor.

He sprawled there, fur sticking out with slobber and human blood, scowling at me.

"If you ever tell anyone about this, I will kill you. And you only have one life. Understood?"

Of course I wouldn't tell. I was a Good Boy.

The light from the floor faded slowly, until the hole was just dirt and old roots and chunks of wood. I snuffled at the edge, but the bad human had gone and taken the smell with him. Just dust and blood and a bit of human urine. The door to the room opened and we looked up in time to see the other human grab the book from the floor and run out.

I sat down next to Cat and watched him go.

"What do we do now?"

He flicked his tail at me. "*I'm* going to bathe for the next several hours. You should probably go home and wait for your human."

Home sounded good. My human sounded better. He headed out the door and I followed him, with one last look back at the hole. We hadn't saved any other pets, and we'd hurt humans, but I still felt like we'd both been Good Boys today. It was a good feeling.

Even better was hours later, when my human came back and found me curled up on the porch. He yelled at me for getting out, but when it was bed time he still put my blanket up on the bed. I'd been keeping my head down from shame. He patted the blanket.

"Come on, buddy. I'm not mad. You didn't run off or cause any trouble." I climbed up next to him and accepted the head scratches.

"All things considered, you did pretty good. Good dog."

It was the only thing I wanted to hear.

The End

Shoshanah Holl is a writer first published in 2013, and an illustrator since she could first hold a crayon. Originally a cornhusker, she now hails from the snowy wilds of Minneapolis, Minnesota. When not taking care of a smug alley cat and a very lazy pit bull, she enjoys horror movies, books, very loud music, and collecting tiki mugs.

http://snhollart.wordpress.com/

GUARDIAN

BY REBECCA MCFARLAND KYLE

I must find the child Coyote ordered me to watch quickly.

Cat-chaser soared above the roofs of many human dwelling-places neatly laid out in squares with fences bordering them. She hoped she could hone in on the sense of magic she sought that sparked intermittently in the chill early spring air.

Soon, the leaden clouds above would drop their burden of rain and the land would be green again and food would be plentiful. Now she would have to work to find food. Good thing humans were wasteful and crow-kind uncommonly clever. She would survive in this new place. She survived enough winters to recall the time when Coyote was young.

She cawed greetings to the local flock, who had remained in their territory through winter. They were presently perched on poles and winter-barren trees and offered friendly responses back. When she asked about the child, they did not know of one possessing magic in the area. They were ordinary corvids which was excellent for her purposes. They would watch for her. They did report food and shinies were abundant and they would welcome another, particularly one sent by the Trickster. She would have a home, but first she forced herself to focus. Find the child, and then feed herself and collect the twigs and shinies to begin her nest close as possible to the child's own.

The Trickster would not be pleased if she dawdled and harm came to his descendent. He did not explain why he took a particular interest in this one, but when a Personage requested one of his creatures to act as a guardian, it was wise to follow through quickly.

Caw! Cat-chaser called out.

She spotted a tiny golden-haired girl riding on a shiny toy horse, and singing sweetly to herself. Was she the one? Cat-chaser didn't sense any power from the heights, so she circled downward preparing to fly closer.

Power from somewhere close by buoyed Cat-chaser's flight. Raw magic tingled her feathers from beak to tail. It carried on the breeze, but did the power come from the girl-child or elsewhere?

CAW! CAW! CAW!

Cat-chaser screeched in alarm and dived. The little girl rode her wheeled toy horse onto the human road in front of a big shiny car.

HONK! The car sounded louder than any angry goose. Cat-chaser rose up in the air, winging as fast as she could away from the deadly front grill. The car screeched as it tried to stop.

A human boy with dark hair the color of a crow's wing, shouted and ran toward the child yelling for her to run.

At the very last, the girl heard the car, turned and screamed at the oncoming vehicle. Her cries cut off when the metal grill struck her with a sickening crunch of shattering bones.

The little girl flew through the air and crashed on the still winter-hard ground near the boy's feet, her toy horse broken in half. Cat-chaser dove toward them just as a man thrust himself between the boy and the fallen girl child.

"Get away!" The man threw his arm in front of the boy and knocked him hard on the ground. Cat-chaser watched as he bent over the child to aid her. His face fell when he felt for breath and found none. Then the man covered the broken child's mouth with his own attempting to breathe his life back into her lungs.

Cat-chaser flew over the girl's body. Scents of hot blood filled her beak. The girl's body lay sprawled, her vivid blue eyes staring lifelessly at the first raindrops drifting down from the leaden skies.

"Get out, Crow!" The man bellowed, his anger and grief hot in the air. He pulled a gun from his jacket. Cat-chaser dodged sideways as he fired the gun in her direction and flew off scolding a curse at him. She landed on a high perch a safe distance from the man with several of the local flock to watch.

Bad man! Bad man! She cawed to the others of the flock who shared the warning to more distant

Rebecca McFarland Kyle

crows for miles around. They would all know his face and he would never find a friend among crow-kind. His own car would be covered with their scat and they would flock and jeer at him whenever he exited his nest.

Cat-chaser's feathers ruffled when she saw the spots where the boy's hands landed on the bare compacted dirt showed the green of spring. Were she a robin, she'd have broken out in joyous song. She'd found Coyote's ancestor and no harm had befallen him. Now she understood why the wily old god was interested in the boy. The Trickster must have bred with a powerful healer.

Fortunately, the humans were far too intent upon the broken girl-child to notice what the boy's spilled magic wrought. The boy himself stood apart, his head bowed, dark eyes focused on the lifeless girl child's body. A single tear traced a damp trail down his cheek.

Cat-chaser bowed her own head. Children, whether they were crow-kind or humans, were precious and to be cherished and protected. She remained watching over the patch of ground and waiting for an opportunity to gobble up the growth perhaps to gain a bit of power from the magic, too. It would be needed if the start of her acquaintance with the boy-child was any indication.

She watched as new vehicles came and removed the dead girl-child from the scene. Pity to waste such tender flesh, particularly the eyes. Humans never understood that the best way to honor Death was to feed Life.

Once the humans cleared the scene, she swooped down along with several members of the local flock to partake of the green patch the boy's touch had made. A fresh scent like what followed spring rain arose from the tiny hand-sized bit of growth. The sweet and succulent green grass was the best she'd ever tasted. Her wings beat faster and her eyes saw clearer than she ever experienced. The flock cawed back and forth with delight.

Cat-chaser followed the wispy trail of magic through the rainfall to the boy's home. A tall pine, perfect for nesting, grew at the back of their property. Though she noted scat from dogs and a cat glowering from an indoor perch at her, she also smelled husks of peanuts someone set out for her kind. She quickly gathered scraps of cast-off human clothing and other warm materials that Fate had scattered on the winds for her nest.

Good humans, the local flock cawed their approval. *Good boy.*

As the sky darkened, she knew she'd found the perfect nest. From her vantage point, she could look into the human dwelling and see the boy's sleeping place. He shared the nest with a fuzzy black-furred pup with prick ears who remained faithfully at his side. He read books, and then set to weaving sinew around a circle of bent wood. She watched intently wondering what magic the web he created within the circle would hold. A completed circle with shiny beads strung in the web and feathers hanging from the bottom hung over his bed.

149

His mother, a tall woman with dark hair and bronze skin like his, came in to tell him it was time he rested. She hugged him and sat by his bedside for a bit, talking quietly. Once she left, the boy was back up, restless in the darkened room, his gaze darting back and forth.

Cat-chaser watched as the boy paced the small space until he fell asleep. He awakened several times crying out. The pup soothed him each time, licking the tears from his face.

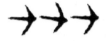

The next morning, the house's back door opened and four dogs poured outside into the fenced back yard. The three eldest were much like the boy's pup, with a silver-muzzled alpha bitch leading the pack. The three paced the yard like good guardians, making sure all was as they'd left it the night before. The pup made the rounds, then rushed to the fence looking up at Cat-Chaser with his bright golden eyes full of curiosity. The boy emerged from the house and stopped the pup from barking.

"Hello, Friend Crow." The boy said, his eyes rising to see her on her high perch in the pine. He looked much like Coyote's two-legged form with his crow's feather dark hair and bronze skin. His eyes were tired from a sleepless night, but his mouth bowed up at the sight of her and she saw the sparks of merriment there passed down from his ancient kinsman. He was still growing, awkwardly tripping over feet that were overlarge for his slender body. The powers he'd inherited had not yet manifested, though she could sense that he would be strong in his gifts. "Welcome."

He set down the bowls for each dog, giving them a pet and a kind word or two, then returned to the house.

Cat-chaser nearly danced on her perch when he returned and tossed out a handful of unshelled peanuts for her. He stood between her and the other dogs, though they were all preoccupied enough with their own food they didn't bother with hers.

The pup crept forward, his tail wagging. His eyes were wide and curious and he almost wriggled with delight and curiosity. He reminded her much of a young fledgling, so full of life and wonder.

I am Cat-Chaser, she cawed softly to the pup. *I am here to watch over the boy.*

I am Lincoln. The pup replied. *He is my boy. It is my job to care for him.*

Cat-Chaser bobbed her head in acknowledgement. Best to use flattery here. *I saw you protect him from dreams last night. You did well.*

It was so cold, Lincoln's gold eyes were wide and his fur rumpled like a frightened cat's. *Joy came to visit, only it wasn't her. She couldn't play or pet me or talk. She scares both of us. She is afraid and alone. I tried to help, but I don't know how.*

I am an old crow and wise for my kind. Cat-Chaser said. *I will help you protect your boy.*

151

The pup paused looking uncertain until the alpha bitch moved forward and bowed her head in acknowledgement. She spoke in a soft voice: *You have our thanks, Wise Crow. Our boy is good and we do not want him to come to any harm.*

Cat-chaser's feathers ruffled. The Trickster possessed a much longer view of events than mere crows. The boy's magic and kindness had drawn the ghost to him and it would be difficult to get the spirit to depart. Even a child's ghost could do far worse than just bad dreams.

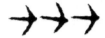

Cat-chaser followed as the boy's mother drove him off to school. Lincoln rode along with him in the back seat. The pup's face was plastered to the window as he grinned sloppily at the whole world.

While the boy was gone, Cat-chaser soared above the neighborhood. Normally, most human dwellings were quiet during the day with only the very young with their caretakers or the very old being home. The big house where the little golden-haired girl had come from was busy. People continually came there bringing delicious smelling food to the family within.

She watched alertly and gathered bits of shinies the people errantly dropped: a bit of pretty ribbon, a piece of bright crinkly foil…nothing went to waste.

A loud crack made her bolt for her nest in the pine tree. Safe at the highest perch, she observed that a car had crashed into a huge old oak tree right next to the spot where the little girl died the day before. Humans had already started tying brightly colored strings and adding other pretties to the tree's branches in honor of the child. Cat-chaser heard them shooing off more than one of her kind from stealing the shinies.

Curious, Cat-chaser winged closer. Soon enough, emergency crews came to rescue the older woman from her metal cocoon. Instinct told her the woman was dead long before the men came to cover her face and take her broken body away.

Men came to plant a new perch right where the golden-haired girl fell. It was sturdy wood, taller than a man with a nice cross-bar perch at the top enclosed with a circle. Cat-chaser and the others of the flock immediately claimed the three prime spots.

The golden-haired child's spirit found the memorial and toys. She haunted the site, playing with the items. Humans stopped, stared, as the ribbons danced without a breeze. They'd walk on, a bit quicker, their eyes deliberately looking anywhere but at what their brains could not acknowledge.

The girl-child routinely taunted drivers. She'd dance out in front of the car and fly up right in the driver's face. Most drivers would gun their engines and drive quickly away, rubbing their eyes.

One woman in a large boxy vehicle ran up on the grass and knocked down the memorial. The girl's human family put the cross right back up and hung more brightly colored ribbons upon it.

Only the animals and the littlest of the humans truly saw the golden-haired ghost. Though the boy was coming of age, his magic enabled him to see the child.

"Hello, Joy." The boy said as he stopped in front of the cross one day. Lincoln, as usual, was on a leash at his side. The pup huddled as close to the boy as he could and inched forward, his body rigid and a spike of fur standing up on his back. The small one did his best to stand in front of his boy, but Cat-chaser saw his tail tucked and him leaning against the lad's legs.

The ghost-girl ran her fingers through the ribbons making them fly every which way.

Lincoln barked a warning. The boy looked down at the dog, his eyes widening with the knowledge that his pet saw the specter as well.

"You've got to stop this, Joy. You're hurting people," the boy said, his voice low and kind. "Mrs. Jenkins could have been badly hurt yesterday—and her baby was in the car."

A bear shaped toy rose up from the pile at the foot of the memorial and smacked the boy hard in the face. He batted the toy down, but his knees shook.

"You're not like this," his voice trembled but he stood firm. "If you don't stop. We'll have to stop you."

A red ribbon came loose from the memorial and tried to tie itself around Lincoln's neck like a collar.

The boy tore the ribbon away from the puppy, threw it, and then picked up his dog and ran into his house.

What do I do, Cat-Chaser? Lincoln greeted her the next morning in the boy's backyard. He appeared anxious, his tail tucked between his legs and his eyes canted to the sides. *My boy still has dreams of the golden-haired girl and she won't leave the tree. He's tried to talk to her again, but she just throws things at him. He's scared she is what killed the old woman driver.*

She did frighten the old woman to death. We're going to have to make her go. Cat-chaser said. *She needs to move on and it's dangerous for the humans.*

Lincoln's tail sunk even further between his legs. *I'm supposed to protect my boy. I can't scare her or bite her. His dreamcatcher is supposed to stop the bad dreams, but it does nothing.*

Shhh. Cat-chaser said as the door to the human dwelling opened and the boy returned with her treat.

"Here you go, Friend Crow," he said as he dropped a generous handful of unshelled peanuts at the base of her pine tree. He added some shinies off to the side: a hair-pin, a coin, and a bit of bright wrapper.

Caw! Cat-chaser cawed to him and dropped an ebon feather, which the boy caught in mid-air.

"Wow, thanks," the boy said and tried to smile. "It's very pretty. I'll make a dreamcatcher with it. I bet it will be the best ever." He walked back into the house, feather in hand. His steps were slow as an old man's, his head was down and he seemed tired for one so young.

We'll think of something. Cat-chaser said to the pup. *And we must do it soon. The ghost will make our boy sick and hurt more drivers.*

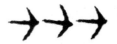

Cat-chaser perched on the open windowsill as the boy wove another circle. Seeing his delight when she'd gifted him with a feather, she'd gathered other shed feathers from the flock and dropped them where he would find them. She cocked her head as he attached three black crow feathers to the bottom of his circular weaving. Power emanated from the making: both from her flock, the flexibility of the willow circle, the sparkling black, gold, and red stones he used as ornaments, the sinew of the animal he used as strings, and the boy's emergent magic every place he touched.

Cat-chaser clawed at the glass separating her from the boy. He startled, then laughed when he saw her at his window.

"Shhhhh, Friend Crow," he said, as he came to the window and raised the glass for her to fly inside. She did so and landed on the table next to his weaving. "I'll get in trouble with Mom if she knows you're inside the house. See what I have done with your gift. Do you approve?"

Cat-chaser bobbed her head once and let out a soft caw.

"Sometimes I think you understand me."

Again, she bobbed her head and cawed once. The boy was actually trying to communicate with her rather than just saying hello. If he would listen and pay attention, she could share Crow Wisdom with him.

"This is a dreamcatcher," he said. "It's supposed to catch bad dreams and help the person sleep." He turned his head and looked at the one over his bed. His eyes were shadowed from restless nights of tossing and turning and bad dreams the ghost had sent him. Cat-chaser had watched as he tossed and turned each night. "I decided I might need a more powerful one so I picked out stones to make it stronger. See, this orange is carnelian for bravery. The gold is tiger's eye, it helps with protection and clarity. The black is onyx, it's for protection. And I'll add the crow feathers you gifted me because crows are really smart. Don't you think this will make a powerful dreamcatcher?"

Cat-chaser cawed once and Lincoln let out a soft whuff.

Lincoln's jaw dropped in a doggy grin when the boy's eyes widened.

"You both understand me?"

Cat-chaser cawed and Lincoln whuffed. She moved closer, sensing the strong power in the weaving. The boy had chosen all the elements as wisely as any crow. She couldn't sense any evidence of Joy's ghost present in his room. The ghost had determined to haunt his sleep. Had he chased her away already with the weaving?

Of course! This is what we need to rid the street of Joy's ghost! Cat-chaser hopped and mantled her feathers with excitement.

Cat-chaser darted forward and grabbed the dreamcatcher in her beak and then took flight.

"What..." the boy made a startled sound.

Lincoln barked and went out the window after her.

Cat-chaser didn't wait for the two to follow. The dreamcatcher weighed her down as she flew over the high fence to the memorial.

She heard the wooden gate to the boy's home creak open and footfalls following her. The three met at the tall wooden pole.

"Why did you..." the boy paused, seeing Cat-chaser trying to hang the weaving atop the rounded memorial. His eyes lit and he stretched and reached up to help.

"You think this will get rid of..."

Cat-chaser cawed a yes.

Joy's ghost picked up a toy horse much like the one she'd ridden the day she died and flung it hard at Cat-chaser. The horse struck her before she could fly clear. Delicate bones cracked as pain struck her along her side. She landed hard on the ground at the foot of the pole. She tried to flutter her wings to take flight, but her broken right wing grounded her.

Cat-chaser fluttered, seeing the toy rise in the air again, the heavy hooves set to strike her.

"No!" The boy cried out. He grabbed the horse and threw it several feet away from the ghost. When Joy came after him, he swept the dreamcatcher through the air. The center weaving bowed when Joy's spirit got snared into the web.

Cat-chaser cawed and Lincoln barked.

The boy stared at the web he'd woven, his eyes dark and filled with tears. His throat worked, but no words came out. He didn't know what to say.

Caw! Cat-chaser urged him. Lincoln made a soft whuff.

"Goodbye, Joy," the boy whispered. "You can't stay here. You're only hurting people. You have to go on now. I know you're angry and lost, but this is not where you belong."

I'm afraid.

The boy nearly dropped the weaving when the little girl's voice whispered on the wind.

I'll go with you, Cat-chaser cawed softly from the ground. *You do not have to be alone.*

"Friend Crow is uncommonly wise and good company," the boy had to swallow to say the words. "She will help you."

Cat-chaser cawed softly and managed to nod her head despite the pain.

I will go if the crow goes with me.

Cat-chaser released her spirit from her tired and aching body, letting it flop down in a discarded pile of bone, blood, and feathers. The ghostly girl watched then loosed her grip on the boy's web and rose with Cat-chaser. They hovered above the scene near the tree-tops, saying a last good-bye to the child's neighborhood.

Lincoln let out a soft howl and the boy sat down with him, holding the dog close to his slender body. Cat-chaser caught a glimpse of his tear-stained face before he buried it in Lincoln's soft fur. His mother came running from their home to see what was happening and wrapped her own arms around the boy, too.

Cat-chaser heard the boy asking if they could bury Friend Crow's body.

"Leave her for the flock," his mother said. "They will tend to her and mourn for her."

Cat-chaser approved the wisdom. They would consume her and continue her mission to watch over the boy and his family. Death sustained life.

Cat-chaser's last sight was the boy with his dog and his mother huddled together watching them rise into the night sky. The boy would be okay. He'd learned two valuable lessons: that life did not end at death and sometimes people were needed to help spirits move on. And that animals could speak. She knew he would do his best to listen.

She rose on with Joy's spirit. The wheel would turn for her: perhaps she would return to the human-place again and live another life. Maybe if she was lucky and she'd been good, she would even come back as something nobler: a dog or even a crow.

Cat-chaser sailed on toward Trickster's lair. From the beginning she'd been his creation to both aid and befuddle humankind depending upon their reaction to her kind. Perhaps she would return to the world of men once again or take some other role in the Coyote's continuing story.

THE END

Born on Friday 13, Rebecca developed an early love for the unusual. Dragons, vampires and all manner of magical beings haunt her thoughts and stir her to the keyboard. She currently lives between the Smoky and Cumberland mountains with her husband and three cats. Her first YA novel, Fanny & Dice, was released on Halloween 2015. In 2017, she will be editing a charity anthology and releasing works in young adult, urban fantasy and dark fantasy. She's working on both short and long fiction on her own and with co-conspirators.

PETRI AND THE SPIRIT WALKER

BY JESSICA BRAWNER

I propped my iPad up on my glass-topped desk's tiny edge and rubbed my eyes, wishing I could will the tiredness and blurry vision away. The oblong black skull sitting next to my computer stared at me with sightless eyes. I ran a finger over one of the prominent brow ridges. The skull was faintly warm to the touch, almost as if it were somehow alive. It wasn't, but Petri, the ghost of a yeti, was tied to it. He and I collaborated—he would tell the stories, and I would edit them and send them to my publisher.

I sighed. *Three iPads in two months, ugh.* Petri's story sales provided a small, steady income, though not enough to cover that kind of extravagance. *Of course, sticking iPads all over the house is a lot cheaper than buying laptops for the same reason. I'm glad we found a text to voice app. It makes things a lot easier.*

Pulling my blanket closer around me, and turning my heating pad up a notch, I pondered. *I hope Mandy doesn't notice how much more expensive it is to heat the house these days either. No matter how warm we set the thermostat, it doesn't get above 60 degrees. Maybe it IS actually broken. I wonder if Petri is messing with the thermostat electronics...*

Mandy was a great live in landlord, laid back, and fun-loving. Winter was her favorite time of year, and she liked to keep the place colder than I did anyway. She may not have noticed the temperature difference. On our last trip out to Breckenridge she went skiing, and I— I had found the skull that sat on my desk and met its inhabitant. Petri had been haunting our hostel from sheer boredom and had been in the Breckenridge area for a long time. After my initial shock at seeing a ghost, and the ghost of a yeti at that, what he had to say was interesting. He convinced me to bring him back to Boulder when we left.

I stared at the curious, oblong skull sitting on my desk and sighed again. *I really should paint it, or decorate it somehow so it's not so macabre. I wonder how Petri would feel about that.*

"Petri? Are you around? I asked.

The temperature in the room dropped another notch and I could see his faint, shaggy outline wavering beside the desk. Words appeared on the iPad and its mechanical voice read without inflection, "Hi Jen! What's up? Are you ready to hear another story?"

I found it interesting that Petri could read, but not speak, and we had tried several experiments to rectify the situation. The lack of inflection from the iPad voice was strange, but I got the impression Petri was eager to tell me another story.

"Yes, Petri, I'd love to." I smiled and then a fit of coughing took over. Holding down a full-time job, a part time job, and keeping up with the writing took its toll, and I had a head-cold. "How did you get the name Petri? Do yetis have names like humans do?"

"Well, hmm. My mother called me 'Petri'… that's what we called the Steller Jays, but I think she called me that because I talked too much. I…" he paused. "I don't actually remember what my given name was."

I sniffled into a Kleenex and sneezed. He looked at me. "Are you okay?"

"Just a head cold," I replied, suddenly wishing for a cup of coffee, or anything hot to drink. Making a mental note to follow up on his comment later I asked, "Is your story an adventure?"

"Well, you'll have to decide. I'd like to tell you about the only time I encountered humans while I was alive. Though I should warn you, it's not a happy story." He paused, looking at me. "Do you still want to hear it?"

"Not all stories have to be happy, Petri. Life includes a variety of emotions," I replied, rubbing my hands together to warm them. "Let me grab a cup of coffee and then you can start."

His translucent, ghostly mouth opened in a toothy grin, and I could see the painting on the wall through his gaping maw. "Very well."

I stood, loathe to leave the warmth of my heating pad, and scurried downstairs. The other benefit to

165

living with Mandy was that there was always coffee in the pot, and it was always good coffee. I poured a cup and splashed some cream and sugar in, hurrying back to my heating pad. I settled in and the iPad starting talking again, while Petri hovered beside the desk.

"How do you humans start your stories? Once upon a time, a long time ago?" The iPad voice lacked inflection, and my neck hairs rose at the eerie quality of it as Petri started his story.

"One year, in late fall, long before humans moved into the Breckenridge area I went exploring further down the mountain than I should. Strange weather is common in the mountains when the seasons change— snow storms blow up without warning, there's a sudden hail storm, that sort of thing. That day, the air crackled crisp and clear, but with a hint of snow scent. Fall weather, pleasant, and still colorful but with a bite to the wind.

I had only seen fifteen summers, young for a yeti, and with as hungry as I had been, it should have been obvious; my final growth spurt was starting. My mother, Oooma, frustrated, would just throw up her paws and send me out to forage in the tundra. That year I was holding on to the season's last warm days with all my might. The cold doesn't bother me, but I enjoy the colors and smells of the other seasons much more.

Traditionally, the forest held more dangers than the tundra, and that day the trees were eerily still. The absence of birdsong would have been deafening, but the squirrels were having a field day yelling at something. Curious, I followed the sound and came across what looked to be a group of strange, bald yeti. Humans. I know that now, but at the time they were new to me. Not a large group, perhaps five or six in all. The only fur I could see sprouted from their head. It flowed down their backs, long and dark, but didn't look like it would keep them very warm. They wore other creature's hides; deer by the smell, one or two had the fur of the black bear draped around them, and each carried a long stick, pointed at one end.

The group followed animal tracks along a path, moving quietly and quickly. I wondered where they hailed from—yeti didn't live in the surrounding mountains as far as I knew."

I interrupted him, "So, you didn't live in the forest?"

"No, we had a cave higher up in the mountains. Our cave was near the peak, up where the snow lingers year-round and the ground never thaws. I had come down to investigate a waterway for fresh fish and late berries, even though my parents told me not to. I wanted to get the last ones before winter."

Despite the iPad's electronic voice, I swear I heard him sigh.

"I should've listened to them. I never should have gone to the lowlands." Semi-transparent in the dim light in my room, Petri's giant paws balled into fists, and his snout contorted into a grimace.

"What happened?" I asked wrapping my hands around my coffee to warm them.

"Well, curiosity got the better of me. I had never seen anything like these creatures before. Nor could I figure out why they were carrying sticks through a forest." He paused for a moment and displayed his massive paws. "I hadn't seen weapons before either. I didn't know what the sticks were. If anything threatened my father he would fight it off with just his paws. I figured all creatures could do the same."

Looking at him, Petri's paws had been strong and versatile in life, twice the size of my own hands, both muscular and dexterous. Now I could see through them, and they were useful only for manipulating the energies of the world around him.

"So, I followed them," he said, picking up the story's thread. "They walked for several days, winding through the foothills and up to the higher elevations, sometimes silent, sometimes jabbering at each other in a strange language. I was careful to stay hidden, not knowing how they might react. At night they would create a camp with a fire in the middle. I had seen forest fires of course, and they were to be feared. These people had tamed it, and the glorious glow in the center fascinated me." He paused, looking to see if he had my attention.

"One night, when they lay down to sleep, I crept into the camp to see how they had trapped the fire beast. Stepping around their prone bodies, I approached. The glowing, wavering, dancing creature appeared to be devouring a pile of wood, within a ring of rocks, but the earth was bare out to the ring. The wood crackled and popped and threw off magical little sparks. Contained like this, I wondered if it was safe to touch, so I reached out and, for a moment, it flickered around my fingers harmlessly. Then my fur caught fire and I howled as it crawled up my arm and tried to eat me." He shrugged as if to say 'what, I was young, I didn't know,' before continuing with his story.

"All around me the sleepers jumped to their feet, grabbing their sticks and yelling gibberish. Frightened, I ran into the woods. The glowing creature edged up my arm further, still trying to devour my paw as I did my best to shake it off.

My chest heaved and I gasped for air, running as fast as I could. I swatted at my arm until the fire went out, but my paw throbbed and burned. Stopping, I looked around, found a small patch of snow and thrust my burning, aching paw into it. Tears leaked from my eyes as I felt the cold relief. The little creature had eaten the fur on the back of my arm, and red angry blisters started to form from its venom.

"Well I won't touch one of *those* again. I wonder how they had it trapped," I said aloud to the night. Sniffling I shook my head. "Perhaps it is like the prickly nettles that don't like to be touched. And I wonder what they were yelling about. Maybe I just surprised them; I did make a lot of noise. I will go apologize in the morning." I curled up behind a large boulder; my paw still packed with snow, and went to sleep.

Examining my paw in the morning, I could see blackened patches of skin, and red, oozing blisters. It hurt. Like nothing I had felt before, but the snow seemed to be helping. Looking up toward the mountain, I could see clouds forming just beyond the peak. Raising my snout to the wind I caught that particular damp, heavy smell that heralds a change in the weather. It would snow in the late afternoon unless the wind shifted. Making my way back down the mountain, I snagged a few pinecones, and found some soft apples overlooked by the bears, for breakfast.

When I reached the campsite, the group looked like a herd of deer about to flee. They jumped at every sound, and their eyes widened with fear as they talked. I had trouble puzzling out what they were agitated about, but when they started walking they followed my flight from the night before.

Nursing my wounded paw, I trailed after them at a distance, cautious and hidden, still curious, but not yet willing to approach. Truth be told, my actions of the night before embarrassed me.

After watching them backtrack my flight for a few hours, I grew bored. The trees were thin here and no underbrush hindered my movements. It was much harder to stay hidden and out of sight. I did smell the brown bear's sharp tang not far away, though he seemed concerned only with filling his belly before winter. Despite the lack of threat, the hunters twitched nervously every time a ground squirrel ran across their path.

When the sun paused in its daily trek, high overhead, I gathered my courage and decided to see if they could answer some questions. I outdistanced them, circled around and picked a spot along my trail to wait.

The leader appeared around a curve in the path in front of my hiding spot. I stepped out from behind a tree and said, "Welcome!" in the yeti tongue, raising my arms high and splaying my fingers to the heavens, but keeping my eyes locked on the group.

He shrieked, startled, and threw his stick at me. It wobbled mid-air. It hadn't been thrown very hard, so I caught it with my good paw. I threw the stick back to him, thinking perhaps they greeted people that way. The stick landed point down with a thud at his feet, swaying back and forth in the earth. It must have been the wrong thing to do. The group scattered in all directions, leaving me scratching my head in puzzlement.

They can't possibly be afraid of me. I wouldn't hurt a fly.

As I pondered, I felt a burning sensation along the back of my calf and reached down to swat at it, expecting to encounter a biting fly. They plagued this area in summer, but were usually gone by late fall. My paw came away bloody. A sliver of wood with a sharp point on it lay on the ground near my heel. Something else hissed near my head, and another arrow flew overhead. A searing pain blossomed in my shoulder. Letting out a yell I ran. They were throwing things at me! And it *hurt*! I decided I wasn't *that* curious about them. Besides, it had been close to a week, my mother would be anxious. Running through the forest, dodging low-hanging branches and brambles I headed for home.

The excruciating pain in my shoulder slowed me down. Stopping to rest for a moment I reached around and discovered one of the small shafts of wood stuck out from my shoulder. I groaned and closed my eyes, steeling myself to pull it free.

It's no worse than a cougar claw, just one yank and its out, deep breaths, you can do this. Shuddering I remembered when Oooma had removed the cougar claw last year. *You're nearly an adult; you can do this.* Squinting my eyes shut and screwing my face up in a grimace, I yanked. The sliver of wood came free and a small spurt of blood trickled out, flowing down my shoulder in a slow, steady stream, matting in my fur. *Oooma will not be pleased about this.*

After resting for a few moments, I started back toward our cave. I had at least two peaks to cross to get home. *Stupid unfriendly people—I didn't want to play with them anyway.*

As the day wore on, my shoulder stiffened, and my paw, already blistered and oozing, screamed in pain every time it brushed against something. My body's right side was *not* happy with me. Under normal circumstances I didn't have trouble traveling after dark with a full moon, but the anticipated snow had started near dusk, and my injuries tired me out more quickly than I expected. Finding a thicket of fir trees near a stream, I washed my shoulder and paw in the cold mountain water, curled up, howled quietly a few times feeling sorry for myself and went to sleep.

The cracking of a twig underfoot woke me. Snow lay on the fir branches above, weighing them to the ground and making it difficult to see out. My shoulder and paw ached fiercely, and I felt my breath catch in my throat. I peered out of my little den, anxious about what I would find.

The stupid, cursed, hairless yetis had followed me. I could see they had mastered the glowing creature in the campsite's center again. Having no desire to encounter it or them, and now wide-awake, I crept out the far side of my hiding place. Moving quietly, I made my way around their camp.

My movements broke open the shoulder wound again, and I started bleeding, leaving a clear trail for any predator in the forest to follow. This worried me. Even my father hesitated to take on the mountain lions, and I was considerably smaller than he. After a few hours walking I rested, watching the sun come up. I fell asleep propped up by the large boulder at my back. When I woke, I could smell the tangy, earthy scent of the hairless yetis nearby. I got to my feet, stiff with sleeping in such an uncomfortable position and turned to find one peering out at me from behind a tree.

He let out a yell and pointed his spear at me. He didn't throw it, but instead backed further into the trees. Without warning, arrows shot from overhanging branches. One hit me in the thigh and another parted my fur, scoring a long line across my skull. Yelling in pain, I ran. The arrows had only nicked me this time, but the thin scores burned and stung and bled.

They followed me all day, sometimes closer, sometimes further away, hurling their arrows at every opportunity and never letting me rest. Managing to dodge the projectiles, I continued onward, but I knew in the high country there would be no place to hide.

I tried to puzzle out what to do, but the pain from my wounds dragged at me, and my mind fogged over. I didn't want to lead them to our cave, but I felt certain my father would know what to do. My mother... She would not be pleased at the state of my fur, or my injuries, or my stupidity.

The snow and colder air seemed to be slowing my stalkers down. When I forded up an icy, swiftly moving stream, they lagged. The cool water helped numb the pain from the wound in my calf and thigh. The rocky banks rose on either side covered in dense low-lying bushes that hid the precipice above. A hunter screamed as he made a misstep and tumbled down the ravine into the water. He thrashed about briefly before the current carried him too far away to hear, swept downstream to a cold end. Hours later, my pursuit nowhere in sight, I struggled up the rocky shore, exhausted.

By midday on the third day I could no longer follow the tree line. Gathering my reserves, I made a break for the windswept alpine. The trees here came only to my waist, short and stubby, stunted by the fierce winds, but still full of the scent of pine. Moving as fast as I dared, I made for the peak. With fresh snow on the ground I left a trail a blindfolded youngling could follow.

Hidden in the boulder field, our cave would normally be difficult for anyone to find, but my bloody paw prints led right to it. I collapsed just inside the entryway.

My mother, startled, turned to look at me. "Son, where have you been? We were worried." Then she looked again and saw my matted bloody fur, and the seeping, blistered wound on my paw and wailed, "Youngling, what happened to you?"

I gave her a pained look and said, "I encountered some creatures in the woods, like us, only hairless. I thought to investigate them, but they attacked me when I said hello. Oooma I'm sorry. I'm not feeling very well. I'm sorry, I didn't know what else to do!" I sniffled, tears filling my eyes.

She sat me down and started cleaning out the wound in my shoulder while I told her about the past several days.

When I told her that I thought they might have followed me all the way home, a worried look crept into her face. She patted my good shoulder and went to look out the cave entrance. Turning back to me she said, "I expect your father will be home soon, he went out looking for you. I have heard of these hairless yetis before. In the stories, they are called humans. No good has ever come from mixing with them. The stories all say they inhabit the lowlands, and come rarely to the peaks."

"I thought humans were just a myth!" I said startled. "Something to scare me as a youngling!"

"Silly Petri, the stories are there for a reason. Humans are not a myth, and are rare, fierce creatures. It sounds like you encountered full-grown ones. Very dangerous. I never would have thought to see them here. Wherever humans appear, bad luck follows."

"Mother," I said, "In their camp they had a small glowing creature. It hurt me. That's what happened to my hand."

She examined the blackened, oozing skin. "In the stories the small glowing creature is their pet. The great summer monster that eats the forests below us—this is its child. You have seen the great beast lick the sky; whose mouth is orange and red, who belches black and white fumes into the air making it hard to breathe. The humans think they have captured and tamed its children, but every so often one of them escapes and devours all within its path."

From outside a great howling arose. My mother and I rushed to the cave entrance. Further down the slope we could see my father. He was surrounded by these... humans. They danced around him, circling and stabbing with their spears. My father, a yeti in his prime, stood eight feet tall, his fur almost the color of new snow. A long shaft stood out from his side, staining his fur crimson. The humans danced just out of reach of his massive arms. One assailant came too close and my father grabbed the smaller creature.

I watched as he bashed its head against the nearest boulder, the blood spray staining the snow. My mother shrieked at this display from her normally gentle mate and ran down the slope to help. Distracted, my father glanced to the cave entrance above. It gave one of the humans an opening to get close enough to stab him. He bellowed in outrage and grabbed his attacker, flinging him across the slope. The other hunters closed in.

Two of them saw my mother and began shooting arrows in her direction. Somehow in the night their numbers had multiplied. Now twelve in total, my father couldn't fight them off. Arrows fell around my mother. I saw one, then two, and then three sprout from her fur. She screamed in pain as red blossoms appeared. My father turned to go to her. As he looked up the slope a hunter speared him in the back. Time slowed as I watched his great body fall.

My mother, bleeding from multiple wounds, stumbled to him. Without a thought, the killers took her as well. I watched the spear fall in a lazy arc before it pierced her chest.

Terror overwhelmed me, fixing me to the spot. At any moment, the hunters would come for me. Alone, young, and wounded, I didn't know what to do. They didn't come. Instead, I watched in horror as they butchered my parents, stripping their fur and skin away and laying it out by the fire to dry. The gruesome sight sickened me, and I stumbled to the back of our cave retching and muffling my sobs. After dark, the smell of burning flesh wafted up to the cave making me gag and retch.

The humans camped there for days feasting and laughing. Why they never came up to the cave I will never know. The smell of my parents' flesh permeated the air. Sick, and now fevered from my wounds, I dared not approach them, but dreamed of having my revenge.

Time was meaningless. The humans left, and it took weeks for me to recover from my wounds. I aged in those weeks, devastated by grief and forced to fend for myself. When I could walk, I said goodbye to my home, touching the paintings my mother had made of fantastical creatures running in herds on the chamber walls. I made my way down the mountain following a scent and tracks weeks old. The trail led out through the lower foothills towards the plains. Wary now, and fearful, I journeyed as silently and carefully as I could.

As I traveled down from the peaks the weather surprised me. Late apples clung to the trees, and winter was still mild. I found a camp filled with these 'humans' near a large stream at the base of the foothills.

A white and frenzied rage filled me. I watched them for days, unable to tear myself away even to eat. My mother spoke the truth when she said the ones my size were full-grown. Smaller humans ran around in groups tumbling and shoving each other like cubs at play. Noting how they would leave at dawn to hunt fish in the streams, I would sometimes follow them. Day by day my anger grew, hot and vengeful. How could they go about their normal lives when they had butchered and eaten my parents?

Late one night after watching for a week, a skunk invaded the cave I used for sleeping, chasing me out, so I found a fir tree. Its branches spread low to the ground creating a nice little shelter. As I prepared to sleep I disturbed a family of squirrels who pelted me with fir cones and chittered in annoyance. Covering my head with my arms I resolved to ignore them, but could not get to sleep with their insistent pelting.

The next morning, I woke in a foul temper. The stream burbled merrily over the rocks and I could see fish swimming in the deep pools. My hunger caught up with me and I tried to catch a few with no luck.

Jen, I have to admit to you, it was not my finest moment. Hurt, angry, hungry and exhausted, I missed my parents. I wanted to hurt those who had hurt me more than anything else, but I couldn't take on the entire village all at once.

A youngling in the village died. I don't know what happened to it, but one day I heard a great wailing. There was a great crowd gathered around one of the small bodies, and in the crowd, I recognized one of the hunters. All of the fury and horror came crashing back. He was so close I could smell him and I wanted to tear him limb from limb. The memory of my mother's dying screams echoed in my skull, and the image of her being skinned and dismembered floated before my eyes.

In the weeks of travel, I had grown, standing now as tall as my father had been. I dwarfed my mother's killer, and I wanted my revenge. He was standing on the very edge of the crowd. From the bushes, I reached out and grabbed him, wrapping my paws around his neck from behind. I dragged him away, the sound of his struggles muffled by the wailing of the females.

I didn't kill him immediately. I pulled him into the forest, transferring my grip from his neck to his arm. A mile up I found a sturdy tree and tied him to it using the cloth from about his waist. Waiting for him to wake up I examined the spear he had been carrying. It had a stone tip, honed to a fearsome sharpness.

He woke late in the day. I looked up to find his black eyes watching me, observing my every move. Taking up the stick I set the point of it against his chest and pressed until a trickle of blood ran down. "Why?" I asked. Digging the point in harder I continued, "Why did you attack me?" I jabbed him again. "Why did you follow me?" I dragged the sharp stone across his chest, leaving behind it a thin trail of blood. "Why did you kill my parents?" I wailed.

He looked at me without comprehension, his eyes filling with fear. Then he jabbered something at me in that peculiar tongue while he struggled to get free. I couldn't understand him any more than he could understand me. "Why!" I raged. "We did nothing to you! Nothing!"

His eyes widened again as I cocked my arm and threw his spear at him with all of the force I could muster. It took him full in the chest, piercing his body and embedding itself up to the shaft. Slowly the light in his eyes went out, and he hung limp, held up only by the spear.

I learned then, what it meant to kill. I felt powerful, and for a brief moment, I thought it would make the pain go away. I hunted down the remaining humans responsible for the deaths of my parents. Every week I would take one from the village and leave him impaled with his own spear, tied to a tree by his loincloth. I turned away from the teachings of my parents—to kill only when threatened, and I embraced the violence. It helped me forget. For a time.

Even in my madness, I only sought out those who had participated in my parent's massacre, but the humans didn't know that. The villagers cowered in their shelters fearful they would be next. The whole place reeked of it. They started leaving offerings to try and placate the 'forest gods'. When I found the final one, the tenth, and impaled him under the snow-laden branches of a pine tree, I could feel the vestiges of what it meant to be yeti stripped from me. The Great Spirit turned his back on me... or perhaps I on him... and I wandered lost in my anger and pain for a long time.

The bittermost point of winter meant nothing to me, nor did the first vestiges of spring. Loneliness and pain stalked me. I thought about throwing myself from the highest mountain peak to end it all. And yet, I couldn't bring myself to do something so final. Winter had turned to spring, to summer, to fall and had then come again in the way of things. I found myself drawn back to the village. Call it morbid curiosity.

Late in the winter I made my way down the mountain. A heavy layer of snow lay on the ground, and the circle of shelters looked as I remembered, though there seemed to be fewer humans about. Scrawny and malnourished, it looked like life had been hard on them.

I found my cave from the previous year. No bears had moved in, and the skunk was long gone so I took some time exploring farther back. I roved purposeless, deeper and deeper into the mountain, ignoring the wonders around me until my foot splashed into a puddle of hot water.

Shaking myself into awareness I looked around. A hot spring burbled from deep in the earth, and a metallic, mineral tang tinged the air. A dim glow emanated from crevices and rocks around the chamber. Luminescent mushrooms and low-growing, lichen like fungi grew in profusion.

Further searching showed an otherwise empty cave and in one wall I found a niche the perfect size for sleeping. I bathed for the first time in months, and gathered several of the mushrooms to satisfy my appetite. As I drifted into sleep, a misty haze settled over everything.

I was flying. The tips of my fur skimmed the tops of the pine trees. I could see for miles in all directions. Below me was the human settlement. My vision contracted and focused down to a tree with a man impaled by a spear. I could see my younger self, tormenting the man. I looked on in horror, remembering.

A voice spoke, its tones all around me, filling me with sadness. "Yeti, you betrayed the natural order, killing for vengeance, not protection. You have had a year and more, now see the results of your handiwork." It took me then, to each of the ten men and made me watch as I killed them. This time I could understand their tongue, hear as they plead for mercy, hear as they prayed to the Great Spirit and asked me to spare their children. Aghast, tears poured down my cheeks.

The spirit took me to the village, flying along the treetops until we hovered over the center. It made me watch as the year sped by for the villagers. I saw children starve without their fathers, mothers weep as their children died, and saw the horror I had created. The spirit spoke, "The humans were wrong to murder your family Petri, but you see now what horror your vengeance has created. This must stop."

I covered my face with my paws, ashamed.

"Petri, you must make amends, and you must teach them to be better as well. You have found my sacred cave, and come to my call, though you did not know it. As long as the tribe lives by this cave, you must protect them. You will not find this an easy task. The world is changing once again and you will be part of it. You must complete the journey of your life and then return to me."

My dream self nodded and the wind rushed past my ears once more.

"Remember, Petri, you must return to me when your life's journey is complete."

"How will I know, great spirit?" I replied, sobbing.

"You will know. Now wake and return at the appointed time."

I woke, lying in the niche, the booming voice echoing through the chamber of my skull and fading to memory. Feeling as if I had come out of a deep dream, I made my way out of the mystical cave and back toward the entrance. I sat and thought, my head still buzzing.

The Great Spirit didn't speak often, but when he did, only the foolish ignored him. Having seen what effect my killing spree had had on the village, I also felt the need to make amends. *Well, they appeared to be starving. I should find out first what they eat... besides me.* I remembered they fished the river—that would be my first offering to them.

Feeling lighter now that the madness had left me, I left the cave in search of fish. I still wasn't quite sure what the Great Spirit meant about 'when I finished my life's journey' and it sounded rather ominous, so I pushed it to the back of my thoughts.

Ice covered the fishing hole, but the current from the stream kept the center channel free and flowing. I cracked the ice with my paws, difficult but not impossible, and set about to tickle some fish. The colder temperatures made the fish slower and easier to catch, but it wasn't pleasant.

I was so intent on my fishing that I didn't hear them. Two boys surprised me from behind throwing a net woven of bark and vines over me. I struggled, thrashing about trying to escape. My struggles threw one of the boys into the icy river. I saw him hit and as I watched, the ice cracked beneath him. He plunged into the swiftly moving stream, disappearing in a heartbeat.

Tangled in the net, I lunged out to reach him, plunging my paw into the icy water. I managed to grab the fur on top of his head. As I held on to him I felt a searing pain in my back and blood began gushing out at an alarming rate, staining the snow and the ice around me. Despite the pain, I worked to pull the youngling from the water.

With a great heave, I drew him from beneath the ice, and then freed myself from the entangling net. The youngling who had speared me looked on in horror, thinking no doubt I meant to eat them both. As my strength failed I dragged the unconscious form to the banks. The youngling on shore ran away as I approached.

I left the limp body near my pile of fish hoping it would be found in time and I struggled back to the only safe place I knew… the cave. Behind me, a trail of bloody paw prints marked my path, and flecks of blood spotted the snow. I grew weaker by the moment, as hot blood poured out of the wound. The youngling had struck a lucky blow, cutting into a major vein on my back.

Lying on my bier, surrounded by darkness and the soft glow of phosphorescent mushrooms, I passed from this world to the next. And thus you found my body with the spearhead that killed me still amongst my bones."

Rubbing my hands together for warmth, I wished I could I reach out to touch his arm. "Petri that's terrible! To die alone in the dark, how did you bear it?" I asked, my eyes full of unshed tears.

"The Great Spirit waited for me. I was not alone." He smiled remembering.

"Petri, your death was partial payment for your crimes. To fulfill your destiny, your spirit will inhabit this place, tied to your bones. You will guard the tribe and be their protector." The Great Spirit's voice boomed around me, comforting, yet stern.

I did much good for the tribe in the years that followed. The young boy I saved became a Spirit Walker. They named him Silence of the Forest and he could always see me, whether I willed it or not. The son of my first victim is the one that killed me and gained his name. He became Snow Wolf, a fierce war leader.

Until they were grown, I watched over the tribe, scaring game down to where they could hunt it, keeping the few large predators away from the village, and discouraging the bears. As time went on the village re-populated and the two boys became great leaders. They took wives and had many children, though only one of Silence of the Forrest's children could see me."

"Do you know if any of their descendants are still alive today?" I asked.

"I would have no way of knowing. When the tribe moved, they never came back. I think that Silence of the Forrest thought I would come with them, but I never told him about my bones. After they left the area other people moved in, looking for gold and silver. An exciting time, but perhaps a story better suited for another day."

The End

Jessica Brawner sprouted in the wilds of South Texas and plotted ways to spend her life traveling the world. She has been remarkably successful at that endeavor, and is now based in the Los Angeles area. In 2001 she discovered the wonders of Science Fiction and Fantasy conventions and has spent the years since working as a booth babe, volunteering for bands and vendors at conventions all over the country. She has taken those experiences and written a book: *Charisma +1: The Guide to Convention Etiquette for Gamers, Geeks, and the Socially Awkward* published in 2014 by WordFire Press, followed by *The Official Dragon Con Survival Guide* also by WordFire Press, 2015.

At the beginning of 2016 she edited her second anthology, *A Baker's Dozen of Magic*, published by Story of the Month Club. She is currently working on her first full length Steampunk novel following the adventures of Captain Jac.

In addition to her convention activities, Ms. Brawner is on the Executive Board of the non-profit Stories for Students, works as a public speaker and workshop presenter on a variety of topics, has developed and taught self-defense classes, worked as an event planner, an entertainment agent, a computer teacher, and a personal assistant.

Other non-fiction publications include: *Booking the Library: A Guide for Entertainers, Musicians, Speakers & Authors.*

Ms. Brawner's fiction has appeared in Steampunk Trails II (2014), the anthology, *Steampunk:The Other Worlds* released by Villainous Press in 2015, and *Madness, Machines and Magic,* the 2014 Story of the Month Club anthology.

When recently asked "When do you sleep?" her response was, "I get a full 8 hours, on days that don't end in 'y'."

You can find her online on Twitter (@JABrawner) on Facebook facebook.com/jabrawner or on the web at www.jessicabrawner.com

CLYDE AND THE GHOST CAT

BY JAMIE FERGUSON

Clyde sulked under the bed for the first few days following the move, but after a couple of weeks he decided he liked the house.

The scents of floor polish and fresh paint tickled his nose, but they were fading with each day, unlike the smells of asphalt and car exhaust that had been ever-present at their old apartment. He didn't enjoy sharpening his claws on the thin carpet nearly as much as he had on the thick rugs at the old place. But the new house had windows had comfortable wooden sills the perfect size for a cat to sit on, which made watching birds and squirrels and bunny rabbits much easier.

He sat at the front window and watched a fat, brown squirrel for a while after his people left for the day, and then knocked a piece of paper off a desk and watched it fall lazily to the floor. It was time for a bath and a nap in the sun.

And by now the sunlight would have warmed his favorite spot on the sofa.

He padded across the living room carpet, and then glanced up and froze, his hackles rising.

On the sofa, in Clyde's spot in the sun, lay a small calico cat.

Who was this? *He* was the cat of the house!

Clyde flattened his ears and arched his back, his fur bristling. He knew he looked fierce—he'd scared away birds and squirrels countless times through the window, and once had frightened a raccoon.

"Who are you?" he yowled. "This is *my* house, and that is *my* sun spot." His tail moved back and forth. He hadn't smelled another cat since they'd moved in. How could he have missed her?

The calico lifted her head and met his gaze. Her amber eyes were dark in the white and orange splotches on her face.

He could see the checked pattern of the sofa cushion through her fur.

Clyde jumped sideways, his legs stiff, and hissed. This wasn't just a strange cat in his house!

It was a ghost!

The ghost yawned and stretched out her front legs, flexing her little paws. He could see the rosy pink skin of her toe pads. She stretched out on her side, as relaxed as if Clyde weren't there at all. Sunlight streamed in through the window and sparkled off the white hairs on her belly. She closed her eyes and lay still.

Clyde stared at her.

After a few minutes, his fur flattened against his body. He sat down and licked one of his front legs, trying to act unconcerned. He shot a glance at the calico.

One of her paws twitched, as if she were chasing something in a dream.

The ghost was apparently not going to leave.

And he was not going to get to lie on his favorite cushion in the sun.

Clyde's eyes narrowed. He stood up and headed out of the room, his whiskers bristling and his head held high. He'd act as if he didn't care. That would show her.

He paused at the doorway and looked over his shoulder. The ghost cat hadn't moved. The sunlight streaming in through the tall windows shone on the spot—*his* spot—on the sofa. It looked warm, cozy, inviting.

He *could* lie on the floor, where the sun shone on the carpet near the base of the couch.

But every time he looked up, he'd see her in *his* spot.

His tail swished back and forth. The sun wouldn't reach the other side of the house for hours, but at least lying against the pillows on his people's bed would be comfortable.

Although not nearly as comfortable as lying in the warm sunshine.

Clyde flicked the tip of his tail and walked out of the living room, resisting the urge to peek back at his stolen sun spot.

Back at their old apartment, Clyde had sometimes managed to sneak out on the balcony to watch the birds, but that hadn't been nearly as fun as sitting next to the window screen staring out at the grass in the yard behind the new house.

Clyde often spent hours looking out the window, watching the birds hop around and eat bugs and fluff their feathers, safe in the delusion that he couldn't get to them. They didn't realize that he always found a way out, sooner or later. The only thing that detracted from the experience was the ghost cat. He would occasionally look up to see the interloper sitting at the next windowpane, her back turned to him.

The first few times he saw her in his perfect backyard viewing spot he walked away, his head and tail held high, twitching the tip of his tail with disdain. But his expression of affronted dignity didn't stop her. In fact, she showed up so frequently he lost hours of bird watching.

He tried to ignore her. He'd turn his back to the ghost, clean his toes, whatever seemed to be an appropriate way to make her irrelevance clear to her.

She continued to appear whenever his people weren't around.

He couldn't even enjoy the fancy scratching post his people had gotten him because whenever he tried to sharpen his claws he'd look up to see the ghost sitting on top of the post, staring down at him.

And every morning, no matter how early he went in to the living room, he'd find her lying on the sofa in his spot.

Clyde even tried going to the living room before

dawn, or on cloudy or rainy days. But no matter what he did, every single time he wanted to lie on the sofa—*his* sofa!—he'd find her lying there.

The only time Clyde could relax was when his people were home.

And even then, he knew she lurked just out of their sight.

Finally, one evening his people sat at the dinner table eating something that smelled peppery and unappetizing. Clyde rubbed the side of his head against his woman's leg, and then walked over to his scratching post.

Out of the corner of his eye he glimpsed a flash of mottled white and black and orange fur. He turned and watched the ghost cat saunter across the carpet, hidden from his people's sight by the dining room wall. She batted at the new catnip mouse he'd left on the living room floor. Her paw couldn't move it, of course, but still...

That was *his* toy mouse.

Clyde's eyes narrowed. Enough was enough.

He slunk low to the ground and headed toward the calico, his pace as slow and stealthy as if he stalked a bird.

Behind him, Clyde's man made a comment about Clyde's toy-hunting abilities. Both his people laughed.

Clyde's left ear twitched. Let them think this was just a game. They had no idea what he actually hunted.

The ghost leapt into the air and pounced on Clyde's mouse. Clyde continued his steady creep. He slowed down to a crawl, his eyes fixed on the ghost as she played with his toy. His muscles tensed, and then he sprinted toward her, running as fast as he could across the carpet. He leapt, as if he were tackling another cat...

And tumbled to a stop.

His paws had gone *right through the ghost.*

Clyde turned around and looked at the calico. Her amber eyes fixed on his, her gaze unwavering and unblinking.

She reached out a paw and rested it on top of his mouse.

The next morning Clyde sat in the window and looked out at his back yard. A warm summer breeze blew in through the screen, carrying the scents of lavender, fresh mown grass, and the tantalizing aroma of the catnip patch at the edge of the garden.

Both of his people were pulling weeds, a task he would rather have supervised from the shade of the tomato plants, but his people were on guard after he snuck outside and scaled the cedar fence a few days before.

Eventually they'd forget and become lax, like they always did, and he'd get out again. He just wanted to explore a little, like any self-respecting cat would.

He spied a squirrel sitting on the top of the fence in the shade of the linden tree. Clyde caught his breath and froze.

The squirrel met his eyes and jerked its bushy tail back and forth. It made a chattering sound, taunting Clyde as if it knew he couldn't get out of the house to chase after it, and then turned around and scampered up the trunk of the tree.

Clyde yawned. The squirrel's day would come. Just not today.

His people trudged over from the garden and sprawled out on the metal chairs that sat in the shade of a big umbrella.

"Hey Clyde!" his man said, waggling his dirty fingertips toward the window. "Are you enjoying the sunshine?"

Clyde stared at his people. It was obvious he was enjoying the sunshine, but equally obvious that he'd enjoy it a lot more if he could roll around on his back on the patio. Especially if some fresh catnip leaves were scattered about on the concrete.

"I talked to Madge the other day," Clyde's woman said.

"Who's Madge?" his man asked. He took a big swig of iced tea.

"She lives a few houses down," his woman said. "She's the lady who has three little kids."

Clyde made a mental note to avoid Madge's backyard the next time he sneaked outside. It would

195

be easy to spot because even the squirrels would steer clear of that many human children.

"Anyway," his woman said. "She told me the people who lived here before us had a little calico named June."

Clyde's ears perked forward.

"So?" Clyde's man rubbed his forehead on his shoulder, leaving a big stain of sweat on the sleeve of his T-shirt.

"She said June used to like to lie on the towels that came out of the dryer, and one day I guess the door got left open and the cat decided to lie in the dryer, but someone didn't realize she had gotten in there and they turned the dryer on to fluff the towels. By the time they realized what had happened, it was too late."

The fur on Clyde's back rose up. He loved lying on warm laundry, too.

"That's awful," his man said. "I'm glad we brought our own washer and dryer. It would be creepy to know something died in an appliance you were using."

"Yeah," his woman said. "It sounded so sad." She took a sip of her iced tea.

Clyde looked over his shoulder at the sofa. The ghost cat wasn't there, of course, since she never came out when his people were around.

Up until now that had made him happy because he could count on being able to relax when his people were home. But now he felt something else.

He twitched the tip of his tail, and then turned back to the screen and stared out at the garden.

The next morning his people left to do whatever it was they did for most of the week. Clyde took a quick bath, flexing his claws as he cleaned between his toes, and then he walked down the hall into the living room.

The bright morning sun shone in through the tall windows, the golden light streaming down on the sofa where the ghost cat lay curled up in a little ball, her eyes closed.

He walked across his room, his steps slow and graceful. He paused when he reached the couch, and then leapt up, landing on the cushion inches away from the ghost.

Even this close, she had no scent at all.

She opened her eyes, raised her head, and met his gaze. Her pupils shrunk to tiny slits, and she pressed her ears back so they laid flat against her skull.

"Hi," he said. He scratched behind an ear with his hind leg. "My name is Clyde."

Her tail moved, hitting the cushion without making the smacking sound a non-ghost cat's tail would make. She gave a low, soft growl.

Clyde tried to keep his whiskers still, even though he wanted to press them back flat against his face. The ghost couldn't hurt him.

Or at least he didn't think she could.

"I know you're June," he said. He sat down next

to her. It took all his willpower to act calm and keep his hackles from rising. But he'd made up his mind.

The other cat's tail stopped moving. Her muscles tensed. She looked ready to pounce on him.

"I like lying on warm towels too," he said. "Or really anything that just came out of the dryer. That must have been horrible."

June stared at him.

"I'm really sorry," he said. He lay down next to her, careful to keep his eyes on hers. He blinked once, then twice, making sure to blink as slowly as possible.

After a moment, she blinked back. Her ears lifted up.

"How do you know about me?" she asked.

"I heard my people talking about you," Clyde said. "They were sad for you. And for your people."

June looked down at her paws. "My people are gone," she said. "Sometimes I think I should go as well, but I know if I leave I will go somewhere else, somewhere they are not. I can see the way, but I'm not ready to leave. Everything ended so suddenly."

"I'm fine if you stay," he said. "You're welcome here for as long as you'd like. And you can lie in this sun spot on the sofa every morning. I can lie in the part that's on the floor."

June's ears twitched, and then she flexed her front paws, keeping her claws sheathed.

"Why don't you lie up here on the cushion?" she asked. "There's plenty of room. I...I wouldn't mind sharing."

"Only if you're sure," Clyde said.

"I'm sure," June said. "Thank you."

She snuggled up next to him and closed her eyes. His side felt cozy, if a little chilly, where her faint touch pressed up against his side.

Clyde yawned. Maybe June could help him figure out how to open the screen door.

He laid his head on his paws. It was time for his morning nap.

Both Clyde and June began to purr.

The End

Jamie focuses on getting into the minds and hearts of her characters, whether she's writing about a saloon girl in the old west, a man who discovers the barista he's in love with is a naiad, or a ghost who haunts the house she was killed in—even though that house no longer exists. Jamie lives in Colorado, and spends her free time in a futile quest to wear out her two border collies since she hasn't given in and gotten them their own herd of sheep. She's temporarily in between cats, and therefore sneaks them in to many of her stories. You can find her at
http://jamieferguson.com.

Jamie Ferguson

TAKER OF YOUNG

BY DANA BELL

Bells echoed over the water, reaching my ears and causing them to twitch. I found the reflex annoying. I raised one paw and listened intently. A fog horn bellowed, breeching the thick mist shrouding the town. Rancid scents of dead fish invaded my nose and I wanted to retch. I preferred my swimmers live, their cool blood a soothing liquid to quench my thirst.

Daring to move forward, I examined what little I knew of the small town. It had once made its living by the riches of gold, silver, ores, saloons and brothels. The mine flooded as the waters rose, engulfing three sides of the bluff.

When this had happened, none knew. From what I could see, the main street supported a grocery, a doctor's office, a vet clinic, and a few other assorted stores. Farther out near the water's edge stood a sprawling school, the windows dark for the holidays.

On the farthest point sat a light house, its beam piercing the thick damp fog.

Higher on the ridge, their colorful sparkling lights joyful around windows and roof lines, were the houses of those who lived here. Great trees bent to the will of heavy snow and ice covering the ground and barren bushes.

"This way."

I turned my head to gaze at my long-time companion Seti. His bronze, black spotted fur blended into the building's shadow, keeping him invisible to weak human eyes.

"Where must we go?" I doubted I could be seen at all. My short black fur helped me to hide.

"The blue and white marble house." He padded over to me, his head upturned. "There."

Since he pointed it out, I could see it. It didn't stand on the highest point like the Victorian house. The blue marble home sat nearest the ocean's edge.

Seti must have noticed my interest in the Victorian. "The Guardian and her Protector live there overlooking the village."

"Who are they?"

"The Guardian has, since this colony was founded, been the one who kept evil from invading and destroying both the town and its people. The Protector is unknown to her, yet keeps any dark presence from entering her home."

"Why are we going to another home?" It would make more sense to go to the one who needed our help directly.

"That is not where Bast has instructed us to go. You should well know by now, we were made to be her warriors. To protect those who have destinies she wishes to see fulfilled."

Of course I did. I just didn't always understand her methods.

Seti took the lead, trotting up the icy dirt road lined with red and green lights, like the lamp posts I'd seen on history discs, which humans had used during the late Nineteenth Century. As I remembered, then, they'd been filled with gas. I wondered what power source the colonists used.

Dampness invaded my fur. While it didn't chill me, it annoyed instead. I still didn't like getting wet, as most cats don't, despite having been changed by the goddess. Seti and I were Chosen Ones, or a form of vampire, but very unlike the few human ones I'd encountered.

Once we reached the teal door, Seti jumped up the two steps and meowed loudly, his thick tail slowly moving back and forth.

Footsteps behind the door, a human coming to answer our plea.

Brightness as she opened the door, causing my night adjusted eyes to blink. Her red hair haloed in the light from what must be the main room. She wore a long blue dress, decorated in a sea shell pattern. I sniffed, blinking my yellow eyes in surprise. The woman who stood there was not human, rather one who walked the night. Oddly her scent filled my nose with spring wild flowers. Hers was not the normal mix of decay and blood I had become familiar with.

Dana Bell

"She is of Bast," Seti explained, as the woman moved back to allow us entrance.

The room felt warm and pleasant. A fire crackled and I moved to the fireplace and allowed the flames to dry my fur. Several other Chosen Ones were draped over the blue flower print couch and chairs. A couple sat in the window, their heads barely visible among the flowers.

"Welcome," the woman greeted. "You are Seti." She bowed her head. I noticed her pale skin and blue eyes. "You are called Blackie."

I had actually never chosen a name. Most humans tended to call me Blackie, so I just accepted it. I urped in response.

Shuddering wind moaned past the window. A gray kitten jumped out and dashed under the chair. Its smell told me it was not a Chosen One. I wondered why it lived here. Most cats avoided us.

"The rest of its litter is here, in various homes." Seti pulled at his claws. "That is part of why we are here."

I'd grown used to going where Bast sent us. I had not yet had the opportunity to pay my debt to Seti after he saved my mortal life from a poisonous snake. I found I liked his company, and he mine. Often Chosen Ones became solitary. That seemed to be changing as mankind expanded beyond their mother world and settled new ones.

"There is fresh fish in the kitchen." The woman sat slowly down. Several cats scattered to make room for her. "I am Gennie."

204

Seti headed to the open door. I followed taking in the sea theme throughout both rooms. Yellow walls and appliances warmed the kitchen. A bright blue hutch sat against the wall with a matching table. Both had painted orange starfish on them.

Below the large window, fish swam in a bowl. Seti caught one, and drained it. I did the same. Sated, I returned to stand at the door, gazing at the woman. The kitten had curled into her lap, its eyes half closed in pleasure, its purr loud.

"The kitten has a destiny." Seti washed his face. "We are here to save it, its siblings and," he blinked, "other young."

"Who would harm a kitten?"

"This town has a dark presence that haunts it. The Guardian, in the Victorian home, has long tried to keep it safe."

"Not successfully."

"She has, until recently."

The horn again blared, the walls shaking slightly. High pitched scratches raked the kitchen window and I whirled, hissing at the intrusion. I heard my warning echoed from the other Chosen Ones.

"It grows worse." Gennie rose, placing the kitten on the couch. She went up the stairs and I barely heard her footsteps as she crossed the floor above us. A chill air crept back down. Excited yips and clicking nails echoed down and two collies trotted behind the woman as she descended the stairs.

Well, one grown white breasted, long haired brown collie, with a pup of the same coloring. Instead of rushing over to us, they sat beside the couch, although their tails wagged endlessly.

Gennie lightly rested her hand on the dog's head. "This is Sheba and her only surviving pup Shag."

A chill swept through my body. While Gennie had not said it, Seti had, I fully understood the dark presence was taking more than just kittens. Pups were at stake as well. I wondered if this only affected us, or did it take human babies as well?

Seti answered my unasked question. "The Guardian has managed to protect them."

It would be up to us to protect the kittens and pups. I yowled loudly and my body quivered.

Let the hunt begin.

"Where are we going?" I asked as Seti and I climbed the icy road.

"I need to speak with the Protector."

"I thought the Guardian lives here. Should we not speak with her?" My eyes took in the purple Victorian with the blue trim.

"If it were possible." Seti climbed the stairs. "It's best to speak to her Protector."

Seti had already explained why the Guardian had a Protector. I didn't see why we needed to talk to it.

Seti quietly crossed the porch and sat down beside a gray stone gargoyle with a bright red Santa hat on its head. "Hello."

"I look ridiculous, don't I?" a gravelly voice replied. Slowly the gargoyle turned its head. "I wear it to make her happy."

"As a Protector should."

"How may I serve you Chosen One of Bast?"

"How fares the Guardian?"

"She is young. Learning slowly what took her Great Aunt decades to master. She does not hear or know the many magics."

"She was not taught?" Blackie heard the surprise in Seti's tone.

"There was not time." The gargoyle slowly rose, stretching each of its stone legs. "She came from off world months after her Great Aunt passed." The hat slipped slightly. "She has found the doll house village."

"That is good."

I had no idea what that meant and waited to see if I'd be enlightened.

Seti sat down. A good sign because it meant he had something to share. "I lived here when it was built. The first Guardian lived in a log cabin with her husband and two children. He built the doll house for their daughter so her mother could teach," he paused. "I do not remember the girl's name."

"Teach her what," I prompted.

"How to protect the town." He rose. "The dark one discovered its purpose and caused a fire that would have killed them all, had the dogs and cats living there not alerted their people to the danger."

My companion stared at the door. "The doll house village slipped into another dimension."

"Only appearing," the Protector added, "when needed."

A type of magic then perhaps mixed with science, often difficult to separate the two as I had learned through the centuries.

"We are here," Seti informed the Protector, "to save the other young."

The Protector turned its thick neck toward the door, the stained glass reflecting the colorful lights surrounding the frame. "You will need to access the little village. I don't know how you will. It's in the attic and may not be there for you to see."

Seti sniffed. "There are cats here."

The gargoyle smiled. "She has a soft heart." It settled back into its position, once again seeming to be nothing but stone, the hat still on its head.

"Come." Seti perched outside the door and yowled pitifully.

I added my cry to his.

There were steps on the other side of the door and it swung open. A young woman appeared, wrapped in a heavy fluffy housecoat, her dark hair barely visible. "You poor things." She stepped back. "Well, come in."

Playing the part, we both hesitantly entered, our heads darting each direction as if afraid of attack. I could smell the cats and dogs. Somewhere too, a large bird lived.

"This way." We followed her through the house, up two flights of carpeted stairs to the upmost floor. Light flickered in the window. A white wicker lounge sat in the turreted area and several kittens peered down at us, their yellow eyes glittering.

"Food is over there." She pointed toward the back of the house. "I suspect you'll find it on your own." She went back downstairs.

I glanced around. The room had been painted gray. On one wall angels, each in a different pose, perched overlooking the stairs. The rest of the room was dedicated to the ancient art of sewing.

"Is this the attic?" I looked at Seti.

"No." His gaze drifted upwards. He stopped near the back of the room, his eyes resting on a trap door I had not seen. "We need to go up there."

While we are excellent climbers, going up the narrow ladder attached to the wall would be difficult, if not impossible. We certainly couldn't unlock the latch.

Seti's tail twitched. "Since we can't communicate with the guardian, we will need the Protectors help."

Dark had fallen upon the house. Outside the branches clawed the windows, the loud scraping noise frightening the kittens who abandoned their warm huddle on the settee. They crouched underneath, shivering.

Seti sat beneath the attic trap door, cocking his head side to side, as if he listened for rodent scuttles and squeaks.

I remembered their warm filling blood.

A creak on the stairs diverted my attention. My eyes saw a shadowy figure creeping around and across the floor. I started to arch my back and hiss a warning, when I realized it had no smell. This was no dark presence, nor a living creature.

"I would ask how you got into the house," Seti said, turning his head. "But I suspect you have done this many times."

"Many," the Protector agreed. "You need to go up there." He pointed a stone finger at the bolted trap door.

"Fortunate you are more humanoid than animal shaped," Seti said. "You have hands to assist us."

The Protector had pointed ears, and its stone hair, what I could see beneath the hat, seemed wavy. Its gray stone face didn't look human. More like a mythic creature from days long past.

Making no noise despite its heavy stone, the Protector scurried up the wall ladder and undid the bolt. He came back down, then carried first Seti, then myself, up and setting us upon the dusty attic floor. I could see faint human foot prints, no doubt belonging to the Guardian.

"I must return to my perch. You must have the Guardian open the door for you."

"Do as you must," Seti replied.

My thin tail slowly waved back and forth, the mustiness tickling my nose. All around, boxes and furniture leaned against the walls. Wrapping paper lay stacked near the only round window, where the faint twin moons peeked inside.

Seti sat down. "We must wait."

"For what?"

"The tiny village. It's not here."

The Protector had warned us it might not be. I did not understand how it could appear. The space seemed too small.

I had seen tiny villages before, often in forgotten museums. They took up entire, huge rooms.

"How can it appear? There is no space for it." Understanding magic I still haven't mastered.

"It is the magic of the place."

"Our wait could be long." I licked a spot on my shoulder.

"Perhaps," Seti agreed.

"How will its appearing help us?"

"As I remember," Seti jumped up and settled on top of box. "Each home reflects the actions of those who live there, including animals. We should be able to hunt the evil easily, instead of searching the entire town."

A mouse, or scamperer as I prefer to call them, ducked out of a box and twitched its nose at us before disappearing into a crack.

"At least we will not starve," Seti observed.

Nights here are longer than most other worlds. I gazed out the window and watched the humans below. The Guardian spoke with her neighbor, a woman with blond hair and fair skin. Around them frolicked several dogs that probably belonged to them, a long black haired Dachshund, a Scottie dog the same color, and an Irish Setter with her pup.

I watched intently, trying to detect if an arm of darkness reached out for the youngling.

"They are safe with the Guardian." My companion had joined me. "They have adapted well to their world." He licked his paw. "They have two sleeps, going to bed when night falls, rising in the early morning when they go to visit friends, then return to their beds until the sun rises."

After a time, the door below opened and the guardian returned with the Irish Setters and the Scottie.

"What if the Guardian discovers the attic door is open and closes it?"

"Bast will provide."

Of course. Seti always gave me the same reply when I asked a question he did not wish to answer. Not that we had much to fear if we became trapped. We had food and dark places to seek shelter from the sun.

A rustling of my fur, like human fingers, stroked my back. I whirled to see who had come and blinked at the sight before me. Tiny houses with sparkling lights, sitting as they did in the village. Even the lighthouse sat in its place of honor.

Bells sounded yet again, wrapping the attic space in their sound.

Seti padded over the village, gazing in the windows, sniffing, as he does when he hunts.

I had been with Seti long enough to know that there are times when I needed to wait on him and do as he instructed. My eyes watched for movement, any hint the presence we sought prowled.

There!

I hissed. Seti lifted his head. Slowly I stalked my prey, my body low on the floor. Seti matched my movements, coming around the edge of the miniature village. Both of us paused, watching the black blob attempting to ooze through the barn doors where animals in their stalls slept with several young humans in the loft. A doll turned and I could see the tiny chest moving.

So. The tiny town reflects what is happening in the real village. An interesting magic I had never seen before.

"It's after the chicks!" I could see them tucked under their mother's feathers. I wondered how none there could sense the danger.

"We must stop it." Seti put out his paw setting it firmly on the black. I heard a squeal. "Good. We can catch it."

It rolled away from the door and headed for the Victorian dollhouse. We watched as it ascended the hill, stopping at the bottom of the stairs. The Protector sat on the porch, the Santa hat slightly askew.

"It cannot get into the house!" Seti slunk around the tiny town, crouching just inches away and pounced on the blob. It squiggled in his paws.

"How do we stop it?" If it had been rightful prey, we could drain it like a mouse or a fish.

I heard barking. I ran to the window to look out. Sheba ran up the road. How had she gotten out of Gennie' house? The Collie jumped on the shadow. It

213

pushed her back and she landed with a faint thud on the ground. Immediately she leapt to her feet and attacked again.

"How do we weaken it?" I asked.

"I am not sure." Seti griped the blob even harder with his claws. Below a high-pitched wail filled the air. I heard the kittens yowl, the dogs howl, and the bird screech.

I blinked. The Protector hovered outside the window, the hat still on his head.

"The Protector does not fight?" I asked.

"Guards the door only." Seti struggled with the blob. It oozed between his claws almost escaping as it struggled to get to the door, now unprotected.

"Got back to your post!" I ordered the Protector. "Keep it out!" I dashed back to the miniature house to see what happened.

Darting down, the Protector took up its post again. The blob shivered and Sheba attacked, biting the blackness.

I began to hear waves. Where there had been rough flooring, water rippled, mimicking the real town surrounded by water on three sides.

The blob struggled harder, trying to escape. Perhaps it feared the water.

"Can it drown?" I inquired.

"I do not know." Seti began to pull it toward the lighthouse cliff. The tiny doll house dog representing Sheba raced after it.

Seti yanked and pulled, edging closer and closer to the steep edge. I circled around to the lighthouse, standing on the edge, the water so close I could feel and smell its fishy dampness. I wanted to make certain that if our prey escaped, I would be there to catch it.

Seti backed across the floor, dragging the blob as it pulsated and squirmed to escape. He managed to wiggle around, his front claws extended over the cliff's edge. Retracting his claws, he released his prey.

The blob didn't immediately fall. It reached up a black tentacle and wrapped around one brown paw, tugged hard, trying to pull Seti with it.

My companion dug in his other claws, trying to pull back. Seti's hind legs slipped, since nothing was there for him to grip. The momentum thrust him forward toward the cliff edge and the water below.

I jumped, grabbing the blob, my claws ripping its body. I heard it scream as it fell.

My body tumbled through darkness. I could see Seti's head above me, staring down. The next thing I knew, I hit cold water and dropped deeply beneath the waves. I struggled in whirling wet, trying to escape. Not that I would drown. My body would go into a deep sleep until I washed up on shore somewhere. Not that I wanted that to happen.

I pushed hard, hoping to reach the surface. My head pushed through and I wildly looked around trying to figure out where the shore might be. The two moons provided some light, but not enough to help.

A flash of white danced across the waves. I blinked, trying to understand where it came from. There was another and another.

The lighthouse beacon!

I could see the round structure perched on the cliff's edge. I started swimming toward it.

Waves rocked me constantly, trying to pull me further away. I pushed on, hoping I would not be lost in the vast ocean of this world.

Teeth grabbed my neck. I wanted to fight, but my body instinctively went limp. I feared perhaps some predator had claimed me. Granted, I would not die in their belly, but it would be very unpleasant until it spat me out.

I don't know how long it took to reach the shore. The teeth dropped me.

"Good girl, Sheba." A warm towel surrounded my soaked fur. "Easy, Blackie. You're safe." I recognized Gennie's voice.

"Seti?" I panted.

"At my home." Lotus blossoms filled my nose. I rested against the woman as she carried me up the narrow cliff trail and to her home. She placed me before the fire and I let the warmth dry my fur. I was too tired to do it myself.

Seti came to me, giving my head an affectionate lick.

"How did you get out of the attic?" I asked.

"When I realized there were portals, I went to Gennie and asked for her help."

I turned my head to where Gennie rubbed Sheba with a thick blanket. She scratched behind dog's head ear. "Sheba was already in the water searching for you when I arrived. I waited until you were both safe."

"Thank you, Gennie. Bast did well when she chose you."

"Thank you and you're welcome, Blackie." She reached for another blanket and wrapped it around Sheba, having the collie lay down before the fire place. "You have rid us of the darkness that has claimed too many lives. It is we who owe you."

"Bast sends us where we're needed," Seti reminded her.

"And you have earned a rest. You are welcome to stay in my home until the goddess needs you."

"Thank you." Seti turned his attention to me. "It seems you have paid back your debt to me. It meant to destroy me."

Sun light began to creep into the house. Gennie rose and dropped the drapes. "There are many places to sleep. Blackie, I hope you don't mind sharing the fire with Sheba."

"I would be honored."

Sheba wagged her tail.

"I will the sleep the day and in the night, you can give me an answer, Seti and Blackie." Gennie gave Sheba a quick pat on the head.

"We will stay," Seti assured her. "We must make certain the darkness is gone and that all young are safe."

"As it should be." She hurried up the stairs. The kittens of the house scurried after her.

"So," I said, "we are to stay together."

"Unless you are tired of my company."

"I am not." I moved so I could snuggle against Sheba. She put her head down on her paws, her tail thumping the floor. Her pup bounced in and settled next to her.

"They are not ordinary dogs, are they?" I asked Seti.

"They are not." He stretched beside us, one paw touching mine. "They have a long history. Perhaps, tonight, I will tell you."

"I would like that." I rested against Sheba and allowed her breathing to soothe me to sleep.

The End

Dana Bell enjoys writing regional tales and has lived many places including Boston, MA., Idaho and Oregon. Currently residing in Colorado, many of her stories are set there and star the various cats she's been owned by. Her works include her novels *Winter Awakening* and *God's Gift,* a popular cat vampire short story series, and various other tales. She has edited several anthologies including *Of Fur and Fire*, *Time Traveling Coffers, Different Dragons, Different Dragons 2,* and *Supernatural Colorado*. For fun, Dana builds and decorates doll houses. She's still settling into her new home and has managed to kill most of her houseplants.

MORIOR INVICTUS

BY BOOM BAUMGARTNER

I am sitting on a tree branch watching my flockmate, Nonus, come toward me. The morning is wet with a now dissolving fog, and the bark beneath my talons is cold. We are a day's walk from the closest village, so the worn paths I see snaking through the undergrowth are mostly the work of wandering deer. The domestications of man can hardly touch the wild feeling of the forest. Nonus walks like he has no purpose but to take in every detail of the vegetation, to watch the swaying of the leaves in the morning breeze and to smell the dampness of the loam, and I think that is why they used to call him Nonus Vagus, or Nonus the Wanderer.

I like that about him because I like to wander too. Crows don't usually stray too far from their flock, but my flock has walked the entire length of the Italian peninsula.

Now, no one calls him Nonus Vagus, though it still describes him. Instead, they have given him the name Nonus Corvus, and that is because he never goes anywhere without me perched upon his shoulder or flying nearby.

I squawk, letting him know where I am.

"Yes, yes, Monitus. You have been yawping at me since I woke up." He swats at the bugs circling his head in annoyance. "Are you quite sure there is a *lemure* about?"

When he says *lemures*, he means the malevolent dead. They make entire towns sick to their stomachs, frighten lonely people in the night when there is no one around, and feed into the violence of man. They are why I am with Nonus.

I tell him when I sense the dead, and he deals with them.

However, right now, I can't tell him that I don't know if it's *lemure*. It's difficult to communicate with him, so I say "death" in my own language, and let him figure out the rest. Mostly, he understands.

Mostly.

He does not understand it now, though. I crow "death" at him again, and I follow a dark trail that does not settle with the fog. As far as I know, he cannot see it. I move a few trees down, and wait for him to follow, which he does.

Nonus has seen better days. Though his *tunica* is usually travel-stained and wrinkled from our adventures through the *campagna*, it is now torn with a large sullied hole near his right shoulder blade. His olive skin is pale, and the shine in his hair is all but gone even in the morning sunlight.

"I should have liked to slept more this morning," he grumbles. I don't completely comprehend his words, but I think I know what they are about. For me, the sun is always a welcome sight after the dark. I feel safe in the light. It's easier to see. Whereas Nonus... well, I think he would prefer to sleep until the midafternoon and stay up all night. That is when ghosts are the most active.

Nonus catches up with me and I fly on a few more trees, telling him the one word he truly understands. "Death," I call out.

Nonus yawns. "I get it, Monitus."

He is slower than usual today, too. He stumbles as if he has forgotten what his legs are for.

I don't like it. I remember when he was sure-footed, and chased me through the newly made streets of Aventicum to find the spirits of the Helvetii that tormented its residents by making them vomit through the night.

I am proud of Nonus. I am proud of me. We do good in a world where there is not enough.

I am about to move on again when I see a middle-aged man with tanned skin, and black, curly hair approach. His clothes, a red toga, are oddly formal for being out on a morning stroll in a remote part of the foothills just north of Cividale del Friuli. I look back at Nonus, but his eyes are on the ground, watching for any pitfalls that may be littered along his path. He's already lost his balance a few times in his hazy state.

"*Salve*," the man says. Nonus does not reply.

The stranger's eyes are directed at me, and I puff out my feathers in surprise.

"Who are you?" I caw, hopping away at an angle down the branch.

"No one in particular. I'm just out for a walk, *cornicula*," the stranger says.

I squawk a warning to Nonus, but he doesn't understand my words well enough.

"I get it, Monitus!" Nonus shouts. "Death! You sense death!"

I strut a few steps down the branch toward the end to show dominance. I have seen too much of the evil spirit world to be scared, but I have never understood a man's words so fully, and it makes my heart race faster. I caw again, this time to warn Nonus to stay away.

"Monitus, enough!" says Nonus. "I shall be dead from your nagging before we even find the *lemure*!"

Half annoyed with his tone of voice, and half desiring to keep this stranger away from him, I launch myself off the branch and go to the next tree.

"What a tremendous gift you have, *cornicula*," says the man following me, his pace much faster than the exhausted Nonus. Somehow, he stays with me even as Nonus struggles through the underbrush. The stranger moves like a shadow, or a passing cloud.

"What gift?" I ask, cocking my head in curiosity. Then I look back at the dawdling Nonus.

"To deal with the dead."

"All crows can sense the dead even just a little," I reply, preening at my wing feathers, trying to hide my nervousness. "It's not a gift if we can all do it."

222

"I was not speaking of that."

Before Nonus catches up, I soar toward another tree further away. I want to keep Nonus from this interloper. Somehow, the stranger still manages to keep pace with me. I do not quite understand it. He walks, yet there is inkiness to his movements that dissolve in one place and reconstitute in another.

"Who are you?" I ask again because Nonus taught me to be brave. "No spirit or man could ever hurt us," he would say. And for the most part, he was right. There were a few close calls, like when a strong *lemure* sank him into such despair he could hardly move and he nearly starved to death. I had to feed him like a mother crow, and he only snapped out of it when I took his nose between my beak and pinched it.

The strange man ignores my question. "I mean your gift is that you can work together with that young man. Crows are as intelligent as humans, but they speak so differently that one wonders if you will ever understand each other at all."

I do not think myself strange, but I blink to let him know he's right. When I meet other crows, they usually think me strange. Sometimes they comment on my accent, but they always wonder why my flock consisted of just me and a human. "He can't even fly", they would say. Yes, I would think. But he can walk, and while I like flying, I also like watching the countryside slide by as I sit on his shoulder.

I'm not lazy by any means, but I'm no fool either. When you live on the road as we do, any privilege should be exploited and I would be quite tired if I flew the entire time.

"He raised me," I say, feeling those three words would be enough to explain the depth of our relationship. A flock defines who a crow is, after all.

The man raises his eyebrows. "He did? Your flock did not object?"

"I do not know what happened to my flock because I was only an egg when they died." I shake my head in the human way. "Nonus found me and kept me warm until I was ready to hatch. I do not know more than that."

The strange man makes *hmm* noise, but says nothing more.

Nonus reaches the trunk of the tree that I am perched on, and looks up at me. "Where to now, Monitus?"

Startled, I hopped up, my feathers puffed out. I thought Nonus would be a bit slower.

"Is it near?" Nonus asked.

I look at the inky trail that stains the woods. It is darker, which means it is very near, so I caw out "death" again, and fly deeper into the dark forest.

The strange man is still with me, still moving in a way that defies humanity.

"Who are you?" I squawk when I land again. "Why are you here?"

"My name is Viduus, and I am out on a walk."

Viduus is not a Latin name, I think. This man is not Roman. I do not know why this bothers me. One man is much like another after all. I have seen the Romans battle the Helvetii because they were different, but could not understand who was on which side. Nonus and I dealt with their ghosts just the same.

"Tell me about Nonus Corvus Decimius, once called Nonus Vagus." Viduus smiles at me kindly.

"He is my flockmate," I respond because that should say everything. He is my family, and nothing can say more about my respect for him than that.

"Yes." Viduus nods, and crosses his arms. "Tell me a story about him."

When Nonus stops just next to my tree, I fly forward again. The sun warms the morning air, and I can feel the humidity weighing down my feathers. Below, Nonus wipes sweat from his brow.

"Are you just toying with me, Monitus?" Nonus whines.

I croak, irritated with him. I wish he could simply understand me sometimes.

"Yes, yes. I get it." He waves a dismissive hand. "There is death about."

I croak again, because that is not at all what I said.

"Fascinating," Viduus says. "You and your flockmate have an interesting relationship indeed. Pray, tell me more about him."

I stiffen, not sure if I should answer, but can think of no reason not to. "They used to call him Vagus because he was an orphan that wandered," I say, turning my head to look at Viduus in the eyes, but keeping my body at angle to fly away quickly if I need to. "Then he found me. I think because my birth was surrounded by death, I was more sensitive to it. I would tell him when I felt it, and he started to understand what I meant."

Viduus nods. "But where does he come from?"

"Savages from the Alps came down and murdered his family," I say, and Viduus narrows his eyes at that. "I met them. His family. Not alive. They were dead so I don't know if it truly counts. They were full of pain, and cried out to me and Nonus. I showed Nonus where they were, and he dug out a *lapis manalis,* a flowing stone, to help the ghosts go to the underworld. He found it by the burnt remains of his home. From then on, we have traveled. Sometimes we can convert *lemures* into *di manes*. Sometimes, when they are too far gone, we seal them away using Gaulish magic."

"The Romans were never satisfied using just their own gods, were they?" Viduus remarks dryly, his eyes flat and cold as he turns to rest his gaze on Nonus. I don't understand what he means, so I hop up and fly to a tree much further away, but still visible to Nonus.

A sick feeling aches in my wings when I think that maybe this is a foreign spirit that will take revenge on Nonus for simply being Roman.

The man stops with me while I wait for Nonus. "This has been enlightening, *cornicula*. For your sake, though, I hope you do not find what you are looking for."

I stare at him as he walks silently away. The underbrush does not move with him, and I begin to wonder if it is my imagination that conjured him in the first place. *Lemures* do funny things to the mind, if he indeed is one.

I need to hurry to the source, I think, before the dead spirit affects me too much to keep going.

"Do you think someone died out here, Monitus?" asks Nonus, finally reaching me and leaning against the tree. "Robbed and murdered? Died of the elements? Seems awfully far from the road for someone to wander, let alone a murderer and a victim."

I caw twice, and fly to a small clearing.

"How much further?" calls Nonus, his breathing heavy as he runs to catch up.

Not much further, I think. Crows have keen eyes. We can see traces of everything, and follow it to its origin. This is how we sense death. This is how I know where they are for Nonus to find.

The concentration of whirling darkness that I followed settles into a translucent mass by a large rock that sits halfway into a small spring. I turn around, unwilling to look at what is there. I call for Nonus again. "Death! Death! Death!"

"I'm coming!" he shouts, and runs toward me at a lumbering, painful pace. His footsteps slow as he reaches the clearing. "You sense it here?"

The grass is tall, but I know he can see the outline of a body. If anyone were walking by, they might dismiss it for an irregularly shaped rock, and if they walked closer, a drunken man asleep. "*Lemure*?" he asks, waiting for me to squawk an answer. One squawk means yes. Two means no.

"Death. Death." I say.

"So a *di mane*. What a relief."

"Death. Death." I say again because I really don't know. This death is too new. It is undecided. I hope it will not be a *lemure*, but Viduus' appearance puts that into doubt for me. Please don't let it be a *lemure*.

"Make up your mind, Monitus."

I squawk at him impatiently. Why can't he understand?

He squares his shoulders before he walks forward, and I know it's an invitation for me to join him.

"Death. Death." I say and I do not fly over to rest on his shoulder.

"What is with you, Monitus?" His tone is confused and a little worried. He shrugs, and moves forward.

I listen to his careful footsteps, and hear his hands rustling around his pockets for protective charms. Then he stops.

"Is this a joke?" he asks.

"Death. Death." I croak.

I know what he sees. In the clearing lays a man with light brown hair cropped short. His tunic is travel-worn and wrinkled. In the back, there is a hole just below his shoulder blade where a dagger is still wedged, probably stuck between his ribs. The blood that stains his *tunica* has long since turned brown upon touching the air.

"Is this?" Nonus gasps, and I turn to see him fall to his knees.

"Death," I say, heart-broken.

His voice is ragged when he speaks. "It's me?"

"Death," I say, and I don't know how I found my voice. Whatever happened to him was quick. It was too dark to see, but I heard every grisly moment, not fully comprehending the sounds until it was too late.

I spread my wings and glide over to him, trying to keep my eyes averted from his rigid corpse, and maybe trying distract him from himself.

"But who?"

I do not know. His purse is gone, and I remember hearing the jangling sound fading into the darkness of the night. Someone must have been jealous of the shiny objects he carried, and took them to their own nest.

Nonus reaches out to touch me, and his hand glides through my feathers. All I feel is cold, like the chill of a winter breeze cut through me. "Am I a *lemure*?" he asks.

"Death," I say. "Death."

He sighs. "But I am not a *di mane*?" he asks.

"Death. Death."

I do not know. I found his spirit walking the road we traversed yesterday. I feel no hatred in his spirit, but there are no *lapis manalis* around to aid his passage to the underworld. If he does not have a proper burial, I fear he may become a malevolent spirit. Senseless death always makes that happen, especially a senseless death so far from home. I dare not think of all the ghosts than haunted the borders of Parthia, or Caledonia.

Nonus weeps, and I try to hop over to him and preen him with my beak even though I know it will do nothing. I want to comfort him the way he comforts me, but I am alive and I cannot touch the spirit world, only see it. I caw loudly at him, and over his body. I have seen other crows do this when they lose a flockmate, so I do it now. I keep cawing, hoping to hear someone else join in to give him a proper funeral. Maybe this will make him a *di mane*.

"Monitus, I'm so sorry," he weeps. His tears fall from his cheek, but the ground below him remains dry. I wish he weren't sorry. This isn't his fault. This is mine. He named me Monitus to warn him of bad things, and I failed to see the cutpurse that stole not only his shiny things, but his life.

I caw louder in my despair.

We may be the only two of our flock, but I think I am surely enough to mourn him, and help him move on. He reaches for me again, but his hand passes through me as if he were air. He collapses into a ball, his chest heaving, and shouts angrily. "I'm so sorry, Monitus."

I stop cawing in grief abruptly when I realize I may be the one that turns him into a *lemure*. If he regrets leaving me, he will walk this Earth until he is nothing but anger. He will become what he hunted.

"Death, death," I warn him, hoping he'd understand.

"I know," he says quietly. He no longer looks at me, and does not reach for me again.

I continue to caw, trying my best to give him the exequies he will need to move on, but he continues say he's sorry to me through his sobs. No, no, no, I think. Regret will only tie you here.

I cannot stand the thought of Nonus becoming a *lemure*, so I hop toward him, spreading my wings out threateningly. "Stop!" I cry, but he only hears the word "death."

"Are you lost, boy?" a voice says, and I understand it. I hop around to look at Viduus. I pivot and spread my wings out again, trying to defend Nonus from whatever spirit it is.

Nonus hears him too, and he jerks his tear-stained face upward. "What are you?" he asks after a few moments.

When Nonus asks "what" instead of "who", I begin to understand what Viduus may really be, and fold my wings back in. I still watch him warily, unblinkingly.

"Hard to say. *Di Mane*. God. Both, perhaps. Probably both."

Something like confusion and relief wash over Nonus' face, and I feel safer after seeing it. He isn't an evil spirit, but that still doesn't explain his presence.

"I dare say, turning into a *lemure* because you're worried about your friend is quite admirable even if it's also ill-advised and despicable," Viduus says as he finds a rock by the spring and sits on it. "You should know better."

Nonus does not know what to say. I have seen him like this many times before, though usually when a pretty girl talks to him when he stops to ask for directions.

"I've talked to your *cornicula* here," Viduus says, "and I think you deserve more than this." He gestures at Nonus's prone body. "You have done many a good service for the dead, and I wish you to continue."

Nonus turns his face away, and wipes away his tear. "How?" he asks finally.

231

"I am Viduus, an ancient god stolen from the Estrucans and then promptly forgotten." Viduus smiles, but it seems pained. "I separate the souls from their bodies, and free them from their Earthly prison. But I grow tired, and I have been looking for a partner to help guide those who are lost to Hades. Someone who understands death. Understands why someone would want to stay. You are a good man who comprehends fully the necessary path we must take after we are finished living."

"I don't understand," Nonus whispers haltingly. "You're either a *lemure*, or a *di mane*. I've never seen one help separate the soul."

Viduus shrugs. "I'm not really a Roman god, so the rules don't apply to me as much as others. I'm saying I will make you a *di mane*, a god such as myself, to help split the souls of the dead from their bodies and ferry them past their remorse and hatred to the underworld."

Nonus looks over at me. "What about Monitus? He has always helped me. What is his reward?"

"Are you asking for Monitus to die and join you?" asked Viduus, raising his eyebrows in surprise.

Instantly, I stiffen. I do not know how to feel about this. I do not want to be separated from my flock, but I do not want to die either.

"No!" shouts Nonus angrily. "I'm just asking who will be his flock while I am gone?"

Viduus nods his hair, and I am mesmerized by the blue-black color that fluctuates in the sunlight. It reminds me of a raven. "He can be with you until his death, and then after."

Nonus looks over at me. "Monitus, is that okay with you?"

"Death." I say, and hop over to Nonus.

"Then so it shall be," Viduus says.

The air around Nonus shimmers, and his clothes become cleaner and crisper. His pallor dissipates, draining from his skin like water, and his eyes are bright again.

Slowly, experimentally, Nonus holds out his hand to me. I know what he is asking because he has done it since I remember remembering anything, but I am afraid that it will not work. I eye his arm warily.

"It's okay, *cornicula*," says Viduus.

I switch my balance from foot to foot before I get the courage to try. With a flutter of wings, I fly the short distance between us and land... on his arm. It's not warm the way I remember it, but I still find it comforting in its solidity. "Death," I say.

"Is that all you say?" Nonus asks, smiling fondly.

"It's the only word you understand," I reply, cocking my head.

Nonus' eyes grow wide, and then he grins. "Apparently not anymore."

I caw contentedly, and hop up to his shoulder, happy to have my flockmate back and ready to continue our work.

The End

Influenced from a young age by greats like David Bowie, Boom likes to add a little bit of glam to everything she does, from playing the ukulele to writing novels. When she's not turning out stories about witchcraft and werewolves, she is a staff writer for ScienceFiction.com. You can find her other musings at LovingTheAlien.net

FIRST DOG

BY J. A. CAMPBELL

You've been watching them."

I turned from the humans' camp and looked at the newcomer. I felt no fear, though when I looked into his eyes, I saw the night sky filled with stars. Much larger than me, his coat was whiter than the newest snow, but I felt no threat from him, though eye contact was always a threat.

A human made a loud noise and I turned back to watch. "This morning they threw sticks at the water. At first I thought it a dumb game, but then one caught a swimmer. They throw their sticks at the large runners, and sometimes catch them. This is clever. Their fires seem warm when the night is cold, and they make a wide variety of sounds. These humans are worth study."

"You do not hate them?" the strange wolf said.

"No. They only try to survive as we do."

"You do not fear them?"

"Only a little. Only because I do not know them."
I turned to look at the strange wolf again.

"Would you know them better?"

"Who are you?" It seemed odd that I hadn't heard
this large wolf approach. Hadn't smelled him, still
couldn't smell him even though he was down wind.
Strange, too, that I hadn't thought to question him
right away. He was an intruder in my territory. I was
the Alpha of my pack and it was my job to protect my
pack's territory.

The wolf met my eyes, and looking into them I
again saw only the vast, starry sky, and again, there
was no threat, no quest for dominance.

"In many years the humans will give me a name.
They will call me Wepwawet."

Tilting my head, I considered his name. It didn't
mean much to me. The strange wolf must have seen
my confusion because he dropped his jaw in a grin.

"You may call me First Wolf, and you may know
that I am immortal, and that I will look out for your
people through all ages, though rarely will you see
me."

I bowed low. The Keeper of Stories told many
tales of First Wolf.

"No need. We are equal." He pointed his nose
toward the humans. "You wish to know them better."

This time it wasn't a question. "Yes." I sat though
I felt humble and greatly honored that First Wolf
would come to me.

"Very well. Then I will tell you this. If you go to
the humans, in time they will become your brothers,
and your brothers will become your enemies."

I knew he spoke of other wolves.

"Eventually you will call them master and they will call you dog. You will travel with them, hunt with them, work with them, live with them, and die with them. Life will not always be easy, but it will not always be hard. Some will be unbelievably cruel, some exceptionally kind, and many indifferent. Above all you will become their protectors, even when they don't know you are defending them." He paused and met my eyes again.

"I understand."

Amusement danced in his star-filled eyes. "I'm not quite sure you do. Very well. I will give you a hint, and three gifts, should you choose to go among the humans."

"I would know more."

"You are a brave wolf, leader of your pack, and to abandon them would be wrong. I will become wolf and guard your pack and teach the eldest male pup until he is ready to take your place."

I bowed, unable to express how glad that made me any other way. This time he didn't correct me. Perhaps he understood.

"Your next gift is your name. You will be First Dog, though the humans will call you something different. Stories will be sung of you in the wolf world for the rest of time. I will see to it."

That was really two gifts, but I didn't point that out as I sunk lower to the ground, awed with the honor.

"And the last gift comes with a price. You are First Dog, and all that descend from you will be more intelligent and better able to discover, and fight, those threats that form from the darkness and would hunt the humans. The price is that you must use your gift when it is called upon. You, and your descendants must never rest when the darkness hunts the land."

First Wolf spoke of the evil that sometimes infected creatures in the wild and caused them to do unthinkable things, killing their own kind for no reason, running off cliffs, making others around them sick. That I would be able to fight this evil thrilled me.

My belly pressed into the snow, I bowed so low.

"And last, the hint. Humans want you to look them in the eye in friendship, not in threat. Now go, eat from their hand, and be First Dog."

Sitting up, I met First Wolf's eyes one last time, knowing I'd never see their starry depths again. "Would you howl with me so that I can remember being wolf once I live with the humans?"

First wolf tilted his head to the sky and I joined his song. We sang of the wilderness, and the freedom, and then of the life that awaited me as First Dog.

Several Years Later

My human's mate adjusted my pack so that it didn't hurt and she scratched my ears. Accepting her touch, I dropped my jaw in a doggy grin that the humans seemed to appreciate. She grinned back, holding eye contact for a moment before going over to one of my older pups. She too was big enough to carry a pack and would soon have pups of her own. A few more wolves had joined us after I became a dog, but my pups were the most intelligent and the most highly prized.

The first few months were the hardest, accepting touch and eye contact and reprimand when I was slow to catch on to the humans' wishes. The one who invited me into his home simply called me Dog. He and his mate and their pups had names for themselves, guttural grunts and sounds that I had no hope of making, but I could recognize when they spoke about one another.

Learning their body language wasn't as difficult as I had feared, but their words were a challenge. My pups learned much faster than I had, but that was to be expected and made me proud.

We were moving to our winter camp. The snows had come early this year and we weren't as prepared as last season. Putting my nose to the air, I inhaled the scent of another snow. We had a day, maybe less before it hit us. Wolf instincts told me this would be a bad snow, and that we should find a warm den, but I couldn't tell the humans except by whining at the sky, and they didn't understand that. We did have one advantage, we carried our dens with us and we had stores of food.

A lone mournful cry rose in the distance and shortly two others joined the song. One wolf sang of a day of hunting and a recent kill. The others welcomed him back to his den. Part of me ached to raise my head and join their song of the wild but I was First Dog and we had our own songs to sing.

My youngest, who bounced like a small hopper wherever she went, hopped up to me.

"Shouldn't we hide from the snow?"

"Yes, Pup, but the humans don't seem to know. We must keep them safe. Make sure the humans stay together and tell your litter mates to stay with those who know the way.

"Okay." She bounded off.

Giving the sky one more unhappy look, I went over to my humans and sat, waiting until we left.

The snow started slowly at first. A few flakes falling from a cloudy sky. The snow caused a bit of anxiety from the humans, but they decided to continue.

Sighing, I glanced around for my youngest pups. They were all sticking close as I had instructed. Shortly the snow fell thickly and we weren't in a good spot to set up camp, exposed on the mountainside as we were. I knew there were trees up ahead and we pushed on toward those.

"Stay together. Watch the humans," I barked as the wind picked up. I heard answering yips and barks as the other dogs acknowledged my command.

Wind howled around us, driving the snow into our eyes, fur and ears, making it impossible to see and hear. My nose still worked though and the tree scent was strong.

"Follow your nose." I tried to bark above the wind and thought I heard answering barks but I wasn't sure.

The humans had a long rope and many held onto it to try and stay together. I pushed up against my human and his free hand found my ruff.

We were almost there. My human cried out in relief when we made it to the sheltering trees. As soon as we were far enough into the trees the humans hastily put up their shelters. Watching as the rest of our group straggled in, I started to worry when a few didn't appear. Knowing my howl would carry through the storm, I threw back my head and sang 'here we are.'

Others took up my song and soon the missing members of our pack joined us. When we were all accounted for we fell silent and the snow cut us off from the rest of the world. I was grateful when my human had his den set up and while I often preferred to sleep outside, the middle of a snowstorm was not the time. Warmth spread through the den and we all curled up and slept away the storm.

Several days passed before the weather was good enough for us to travel and I sensed we would make it to our winter camp before the next snow fell.

Pups ran and chased each other in the snow and human pups chased the dogs, giggling in delight and glad to be free of the confines of their dens. My human seemed especially pleased with me after several of those who'd been last to find the camp came up to him and spoke happily and pointed at me.

"Songs will be sung of how you saved us," one of the rival males in camp said to me.

Tilting my head, I stared at him, confused.

"Your song saved many lives, First Dog. Mine included. Thank you."

"You are welcome."

He trotted away and my human called me, my pack in his hand.

I watched in pride as my newest pups played in the sun with the human children. Warmth from the sun-warmed rock seeped into my old, aching bones. The sunlight faded slowly and I was content to watch my pack and nap until the chill night air drove me to my human's fire.

I wondered if I would meet First Wolf one last time when I took the final sleep. I wanted to tell him all that I had learned, though I suspected he already knew.

"First Dog."

My eyes snapped open. Swift, my human's son's dog ran toward me. The light had almost faded, though we had some time before true dark.

"What is it, Swift?"

"My human, he's hurt."

I struggled to my feet. "Where?"

Swift pointed with his nose. "But there's something dangerous in the cave. Hopper has already gone to the final sleep.

"Is it a bear?" I had finally learned the human words and we all used them now instead of the old wolf words.

"No. It's…. I don't know. My instinct tells me it is the evil First Wolf told you to guard against."

"Then we must defeat it," I growled. "Find a few more in my line and meet me at the cave. I will follow your scent."

Swift ran off and I forced my aching bones to more speed than I'd attempted in quite some time. Swift's scent wasn't hard to follow and as true dark fell, I reached the cave.

Instantly, I knew Swift was right. The cave was infected with the same evil that made animals do terrible things. I hoped my human's son wasn't infected.

Swift and two others joined me.

Hackles up, I growled. "We must destroy the evil."

Our eyes adjusted quickly to the darkness. A dark figure bent over my human's son's body. Sadness, quickly replaced by rage, consumed me. He had passed into the final sleep. I snarled and launched myself at the creature, followed by the other dogs. It was human shaped though it smelled evil and dead, and I went for the throat. Vile tasting blood poured into my mouth as flesh tore.

"First Dog, you have done very well."

I looked into First Wolf's endless, star-filled eyes and dropped my jaw in a grin.

He grinned back. "You may rest for a time, bravest of all my people, but if you are willing, I have work for you yet."

"Of course, First Wolf."

"I thought you might say that. How do you feel about sheep?"

"Sheep?"

He yipped laughter. "You'll see."

The End

KILLS LIKE RIVER

BY J.L. ZENOR

The pack watched nervously as Bright Sky, the old Velociraptor shaman, made his way up the steep hill, the intelligence in his eyes at odds with the shakiness of his step and the stoop of his old back.

The young Velociraptors froze as they got too close to the ancient shaman, their prey skittering under a shrub on the hillside. Bright Sky leaped and caught the rat. It looked ridiculously small in his large jaw. He eyed the scared young Velociraptors and then tossed it to them to fight over. The move was a show of force from the shaman, letting the pack know that just because he was old and in pain, didn't mean he wasn't quick and deadly. And when those eyes locked onto any of the pack mates, you knew that he was studying you.

Bright Sky reached the top of the hill just as the sun set over the mountains in the distance. The moon was just a sliver this night, already high above the mountains, which somehow made the falling star stand out even more against the backdrop of stars in the sky. The falling star, as Bright Sky had called it, grew larger every night. What had started out the size of a normal star, just a shining dot, was now as large as a mouse that was running across the sky with the other constellations. It even had a small tail behind it.

I watched Bright Sky as he tried to address the pack, but words failed him. He tried to keep all emotion from his snout and eyes, but the smell of fear was thick on the air surrounding him. He looked taller than normal, stretching himself high instead of his usual crouch. The full height was impressive. He was the oldest of the pack, and that made him the tallest. While most Velociraptors were slightly shorter than a human, Bright Sky was taller than any man I had seen.

"Something more than the sky is changing, isn't it?" I said, trying to interpret what I sensed.

He looked at me, his eyes meeting mine, and then nodded.

"The pack will survive," barked one of the Velociraptors. "We always survive."

"We will not survive this," Bright Sky snapped. He looked around at each, and then hung his head. "This is the last gathering of the pack," he whispered.

How could this be the last gathering? There have been gatherings since the first Velociraptors were named, thousands of moons ago; why would we stop? I wanted to ask, but kept silent for fear that I would miss the shaman's quiet words. He spoke so softly that a quiet breeze would drown out his voice.

"The Creator has sent us a sign in the heavens, and has given me a dream. He is angry with what he has made, with what the humans have done. They summon demons and ignore his laws, and all of creation has been corrupted because of it. And for that, he is going to destroy everything and start over with a chosen few from among us."

At this news, the other raptors started a near panic, asking questions, begging for help, pleading that the shaman beg the Creator for a second chance.

But few others knew how bad it really was beyond the mountains. While they enjoyed living in peace in this quiet, protected valley, the world outside was falling to pieces. Demons ran wild, twisting creation and the animals in it into unholy things, and the humans did whatever they wanted to, ignoring the commands of the Creator. They didn't kill just for food, they killed for greed and pride and worse.

I was thankful when the pack accepted me after I found my way here. I couldn't blame them for the relative peace they had lived in, secluded in this valley. Sometimes I wished I was from here and had never needed to be a hunter of demons, watching the unholy creatures slowly kill our pack with each passing moon.

I watched my hatchling as she left the other young raptors and stood next to me, reaching nearly to my belly. Her stripes were just starting to show on her back, which indicated she had reached the age to no longer be considered a hatchling. I smiled. It was a sad smile. Yes, the world would be destroyed, but maybe that was better than her growing up in a world with demons and the evilness of humans. I wondered what would happen if the humans found our valley. They were already so close.

Bright Sky met my eyes as he continued.

"There is still hope," the shaman shouted above the panicked noise of the pack, with the roar more like that of a great hunter than a frail old raptor, and then he waited for the pack to calm down.

"The Creator is angry, and will send the rains to destroy creation. We cannot stop that, but he is saving a few of every type of creature. And we are blessed that one from our pack has been chosen to survive the coming destruction."

Several raptors clawed their way past the others and pushed themselves closer to Bright Sky, as if he would choose them simply because of their closeness to him. But Bright Sky ignored them as he made eye contact again. "River, you have a new pack member to introduce to us?"

The others were confused by the sudden change in topics, but my heart raced as I started to have hope.

"Yes, I have brought my hatchling to the pack to be named and made one of us."

He looked down at the small raptor who shyly hid behind me. "And what is her name?"

This was it, the moment I would give her a name, an identity of her own. It had to be a strong name, one that would stand out among the others during this dark time. I had several picked out, but none of them seemed right anymore. The rain, whatever that was,

was coming to destroy everything. An idea bloomed in my mind; unlikely as it was, it felt right.

"She will be called Saved From The Rain."

The other Velociraptors raised their lips, showing their teeth. I knew what they were thinking. They accepted me into their pack, and when only one pack member would be offered salvation I was arrogant enough to suggest it was my own hatchling. But the decision wasn't mine, and choosing this name for her was a false hope. But it felt like the right thing to say at the time. I ignored them and waited for Bright Sky's response. His was the one that mattered.

He held out his claw toward her, and she cautiously approached. "And indeed she shall be. Rain, you are the one the Creator has chosen."

I hadn't expected Bright Sky to shorten her name, but I should have. The pack I came from gave longer names that were meaningful and important, but this pack usually used a single word for a name. A longer name would only be given to those that were most important, like Bright Sky. It was why this pack simply called me River, instead of my full name. They didn't understand the importance of my full name, they just thought I was trying to mimic the name of a Velociraptor of legend. Their sheltered lives never had to see the acts I had to commit when hunting the demons.

The other raptors went into a blood frenzy and attacked. I roared and tore into the neck of one that had gotten too close to Rain, growling as I used the body as a shield to protect her. Bright Sky stepped past me and faced the pack, the old shaman growling with an anger that I have never seen in him before. I think he scared the pack more than I did even with a half dead pack mate clutched in my jaws.

"Do you dare question the Creator? Who are you to say that he is wrong in how he judges his creation? I suggest you each make any preparations you can. These coming months will be difficult."

After that the pack turned and left, their anger driving them far from the shaman and his Creator. I dropped the raptor I had been holding, relishing in his pain as he cowered on the ground.

Bright Sky turned to me with sadness in his eyes and a hint of anger still in his voice. "Saved from the Rain will be safe, my young one. But you must guide her to Salvation and the preacher. Travel east, and trust in the Creator to guide you."

The east. Such simple words for death. Of all the lands we might have to travel through, why did it have to be there? The land of pure evil, where demons thrive and make even the sands deadly.

Rain had a look of sheer terror on her face. Since the first day that I saw her I knew I would die to protect this little one, I just didn't know that day would come so soon.

The stars that lit up the night sky were a comfort after two full moons of traveling. This far from home the night sky seemed to be the only familiar thing around. Except for the falling star. That was new. The sky grew stranger every night as the star became larger than the moon. I shivered as I looked at it. A star wasn't supposed to have a tail.

The smell of fresh blood filled the air and I knew this would be another day we would have to move in the shadows to avoid the demons. I needed the energy of a full night's rest, but this close to the demons I didn't dare let myself fall into a deep sleep and I kept waking up at every sound and smell. The sleepless nights were getting to me. It was getting hard to tell the difference between the sounds in my head and those that were real. The smell of demons brought up a past that I wanted to forget, and at the same time made me want to lose myself in another demon hunt.

As the sun rose and the mists appeared—giving water and life to the earth that would soon be destroyed—I nudged Rain awake with my snout. I gave a few quiet snorts as she started to rouse and watched her stretch her long neck in a yawn.

She blinked her eyes up at me. "The sun isn't even up yet."

"I know, little one, but we have a rough day ahead of us. Best to get started early. Eat up." I placed the rabbit I had sniffed out earlier in front of her. She stared at it a moment and then reluctantly started to eat it.

My poor Rain, taken from her friends and the rest of the pack, being forced to travel miles every day with her small legs. Sometimes she would let me carry her, but most of the time she wanted to walk on her own. But even as the runt of the pack she tried to prove herself as strong as the others.

An unnatural scream let out in the distance, followed by the cry of a human in pain. Rain quickly finished her breakfast and stood next to me, looking around nervously.

Without a noise, we started moving. The mists brought out the smell of the grasses and fruit from the human's orchard. It smelled nice, but was overwhelming, making it hard to pick up the rotten stench of death that would let me know if a demon was nearby.

Rain sniffed the air, trying to discern the new smells.

"I wish Kills Like River were here," Rain's voice whispered, sounding too loud in the stillness of the air. My heart skipped a beat at the words and I looked around for anything that might have heard.

"But I'm here, Rain. I'll protect you."

"Yeah, but if Kills Like River were here then we wouldn't be sneaking around like scared sheep. He would destroy all the demons so we could walk past their dead bodies. And he could shout and scare away all the demons in the world."

I laughed. "Who told you that?"

"The other Velociraptors. When I was pretending to be Kills Like River from the legends they laughed at me and told me all the ways that I'm weaker than him. How I could never be that great because I was so small, like you. The smallest of the pack."

Anger rose up my chest and heat flushed my neck and snout. I snorted and wanted to tear into the young raptors that would dare insult my hatchling.

"Being small does not mean that you are weak," I snorted. I tried to calm down before continuing. "My hatchling, even the smallest creatures can do great things. Just look at us now. We were chosen for this journey because the Creator has plans for us, despite our size. When the strongest accomplish something, everyone says it's because of their strength, but when those that are seen as weak do something others say is impossible, then everyone knows it was the Creator that worked through them."

Rain let out a snort. "That's just things the grown raptors say to make us feel better, but you don't really believe it."

I felt anger at the accusation, my talons clicking together in agitation. I wanted to refute her claim. I knew she was capable of doing great things, once she put her mind to something. Why would she think such a thing about me?

I opened my jaws to let the little creature know my disagreement with her comment when she spoke, her words making me choke on what I was about to say.

"You don't even think I can hunt for my own food."

My mind raced to make sense of what she had just said. This journey across half the land had been stressful. We had to be quick and stay quiet to not attract attention of demons, or of the human hunters that loved to collect and make trophies out of our large claw. I had done all of the hunting so we could move faster, not because I thought Rain was too small to hunt.

But that wasn't how she saw it.

I looked toward the large star in the sky as it went over the hills to sleep, to grow larger. There wasn't much time left. I looked at Rain, my eyes burning and my chest hurt with a pain that I couldn't describe.

There wasn't much time left with my hatchling, and I knew it. Did I want to spend these last few days just barely surviving, getting to the end as quickly as possible, or did I want to teach Rain, to show her how much I trusted her and give her lasting memories of this painful time. There would be plenty of pain in the future, that pain didn't need to start now. She didn't need a protector and guide. She needed her mom.

I smiled, showing my sharp teeth in a large grin as I leaned down close to her ear. "How about you hunt for lunch. For the both of us?"

Her eyes went wide and her tongue licked the front of her mouth in anticipation of the kill. And I realized, for the first time in many days, I saw her smile. How had I missed that?

Time was too short.

I ate the mouse in a single bite. The small bite of food took a lot longer to gather than we should have allowed, but Rain was proud of her hunt, so I ate the snack with a wide grin. It was worth the extra time to make her feel happy and useful to our journey, but we still had a lot of ground to cover before the sun finished its journey toward the other end of the sky. And with the sun slumbering would come the star, growing larger with every passing day.

Something smelled strange; like the smell of a terrorized creature. "Rain, it's time to go."

She tilted her head at me, probably wondering why my mood had changed so much, but she got up and swallowed the last of the mouse.

We started to leave the small rock outcropping we had hid behind while we ate, but the smell grew stronger. I froze, and Rain mimicked my motion and backed slowly behind the shelter.

A dog cried out in pain in the distance.

I ducked down and whispered, "Rain, stay here."

"Don't go!" She cried. My heart broke at the look of fear in her eyes. She was supposed to be a mighty hunter, not one scared and cowering behind a rock. I could see the shame on her face for feeling that way, but in the demon lands there wasn't much you could do besides hide until you were ready to attack.

"I'm just going to look," I promised her. "I'm not going to leave you."

I heard her claws scratch nervously at the dirt as I rounded the rocks and looked out across the valley. I ducked back into the rock shelter as a dog ran by. It held its back leg up as it tried to run from its pursuers. With the demon hunting packs dead the demons had flourished in this land, for dozens of demonic creatures chased behind the dog, laughing, toying with the poor injured creature.

The demons took every shape imaginable. Some looked almost like humans, but with wings, tougher skin, and horns sticking out of their heads. Others ran on four legs with features that were a strange mix of a dog and a cat. They all reeked of death and evil, a smell that didn't belong in this world. I wondered briefly what this dog had done to attract the attention of so many demons.

The thought of the fight, of the feeling of demon flesh between my teeth made me salivate. My claws twitched with anticipation of slicing through the creatures as I started to run out from the shelter, ready to kill. I felt a tug on my leg and I kicked back before taking a step into the open.

A scream behind me yanked my thoughts from my bloodlust. My hatchling was trying to get up from where I had kicked her into a rock.

"You said you wouldn't leave me!" Rain cried, and in a moment of sheer terror I realized how close I was to losing her, too.

I ran back to her, apologizing and licking the rising lump on the back of her head. Not again, I would not do this again. There was a reason I couldn't give myself over to the rage. Some things were more important than the thrill of the hunt and feeling of killing a demon.

"Come on, let's hide until they are gone."

Rain ran underneath me, keeping physical contact whenever she could. And then I stopped, listening carefully as I sniffed the air. Something had changed with the smell of the demons. Their scent was strong. Stronger than it should have been.

I whirled around, holding my body low, both to protect Rain and set to pounce. Gravel crunched as a demon rounded the corner, twenty paces away. The thing had six legs and a tail like a whip. It's glowing green eyes stared at me as it growled, drool dripping to the ground in large puddles, sizzling wherever it landed. It gave a loud screech, like a twisted version of a howl.

I pounced, digging my claws into its back, biting deep into its neck as it whipped me with its tail several times, and the warm sensation of blood started to trickle down my back, but I held on, twisting my jaw until the thing finally stopped struggling and fell to the ground.

Rain's eyes were wide as she watched me kill the unholy creature. She had seen me hunt before, but that was completely different than the rage that was involved in killing a demon.

The smell of demon blood grew worse. I lifted my snout to the air, trying to judge if it came from the demon under my feet, or from somewhere else.

The sound of a small army rushing into the rock outcropping we were hiding in gave me my answer.

"Rain, RUN!"

She turned and scampered her way up several large boulders with a grace I had never before credited her with. The smaller demons were the first around the bend, not even tall enough to reach my belly. I turned and swatted them with my tail before they knew I was there. Some held on, but most went soaring into the boulders.

More demons rounded the corner, larger, deadlier ones that knew how to fight.

I attacked, trying to be quick with every attack, trying to go straight for a killing strike with each blow.

Several demons went down in the first moments of the attack, but the overwhelming numbers soon took their toll, allowing them to hold me down as the smaller demons rushed past, running straight toward the rock Rain had climbed on top of. I told her to run! Why hadn't she run?

"Why struggle?" Came a deep booming voice, as a demon on two legs and large wings stepped into the passage. He was as tall as two or three raptors standing on top of each other, and he glowed with green markings across his purple skin. "You will be dead before the sun sets no matter what you do."

I struggled to stand, but there were too many of them holding me down.

"The humans have forfeited this world to us, which means you are mine. You will obey."

I fought against the creatures holding down my neck and faced the demon lord. "You will be destroyed with the rest of us. The Creator will not let your kind into Salvation."

The demon lord bent low and sneered, his breath reminding me of rot and death. "And do you think I will let you reach your precious Salvation? No. You will die and after the Creator cleanses the earth of mankind we will rise again and rule this world."

Rain gave a muffled scream before the creatures dragged her away, and I panicked.

Fear like I have never known took over, and I thrashed at every creature trying to hold me down, trying to keep me from my Rain.

I had given up demon hunting because it had become all consuming, taking over my life and requiring more sacrifices than I was willing to make. But now I needed that obsession, I needed to remember the skills I had forgotten, find those memories of how I used to fight, or else all would be lost.

I would not lose another hatchling. I would not lose my Rain.

The demons forced me back against a wall of boulders and attacked, a smaller one hanging off my throat while a larger demon wrapped its claws around my head. The demon lord laughed at my struggle and Rain cried out in pain and then went silent.

The world around me went quiet as I shut out every sound except for Rain, but I heard nothing. My head hit the ground, hard, under the force of the demon attack. I was out numbered, I couldn't fight back. There was only one way to survive, by unleashing a part of me that I had hidden away since the days of legends.

I gasped for air, breathing as deeply as I could despite the pain of demonic teeth cutting into my throat, and I Roared.

Not just a roar like a lion or a Tyrannosaurus, intended to scare or intimidate. This Roar was deeper, coming from deep inside where the soul and spirit resided. The sound wasn't so loud it hurt your ears, but it was low and deep and vibrated with such violence that it could be felt deep inside. It was a Roar that could make men sink to their knees in tears, as they realized just how much their souls had been corrupted by their choices. But it was worse for demons.

The dust on the ground flew out from me in a circle as the Roar reached the demons, shattering them into countless smaller pieces, tearing them apart by the dozens.

The demon lord flared out his wings in anger at the sight of his host of demons being ripped to dust and blown away with the wind. "You have the Roar? I WILL DESTROY YOU!" He reached his hand down to grab at my chest, but I ducked under the massive claw that moved quicker than it had any right to for its size. I rolled on the ground, the sand stinging as it found its way into the open wounds on my back.

The blood lust took over, driving me to want to fight the demon even though I knew I couldn't win. I leaped onto its arm, took two quick steps up his biceps and then jumped and sank my teeth into his neck.

He threw me off like a pesky fly, smashing me into a boulder. Somewhere in the back of my mind I thought of Rain, and how I should be helping her instead of fighting this fight, but my anger drove me on.

The dog I saw earlier ran underneath the demon and smashed into me, throwing me off balance. I growled and snapped at him, but he was ignoring me and focused on the demon lord, staring, unblinking with its head low.

The demon lord's face twisted in rage, but it didn't move.

"Quickly," the dog shouted, "get your young one and get out of here. I'll hold him with my Eye. Go!"

I stared at him in confusion. I had known there were other creatures that had rare supernatural abilities but I had never heard of one in a creature so small. I didn't know how the Eye worked and at that moment I didn't care. All I knew was that the demon was holding still and I had a chance to kill it.

"No!" The dog barked as I started toward the demon lord. "I can't hold him if you attack."

I growled, not caring. It was a demon, an abomination to all things natural, and I had to destroy it.

"Go save your hatchling!" He barked. "Take her to Salvation before the star falls."

Hatchling? Rain! I felt ashamed as I remembered her. I had done it again, I was on the verge of losing Rain because I was consumed by the blood lust of the demon hunt. Just like I lost Mist. I had lost myself completely to the blood lust then, furious that I had been lured into the trap, that I didn't pay attention as they brought the rest of my pack. I could have saved them, but there were demons to kill!

If the rest of the pack couldn't fight off the demons that had captured them then they would have to wait until I finished. I'd save the pack later.

But later was too late.

I remembered Mist sneaking up on her prey in the grass, as silent as the mist that watered the ground. She was always quiet. Even then, watching me tear through demons to get to the hoard's leader. So lost in my own rage and blood lust that I never stopped to notice as they killed my pack, one at a time. So lost in rage that I never stopped to notice as they killed my Mist.

Protecting Rain was more important than killing this demon. I looked back at the other end of the opening at where Rain lay, held down by motionless smaller demons that were captivated by the fight.

I charged and they scattered, trying to find any way to escape my wrath. They failed.

My claws made quick work of the small demons while Rain watched in horror. I felt crushed that she had to face such demonic gore by her own mother's claws.

"You are Kills Like River!" She shouted.

I looked down at her, heartbroken that she knew my secret, that she knew the stories and knew what I had sacrificed for my bloodlust, trading my own hatchling for the thrill of killing demons; what being the best had really cost me.

But she grinned, her row of sharp teeth showing. "Does that mean I can be an awesome demon killer just like you?"

The comment caught me off my guard and tears rolled down my snout. I couldn't help but laugh. She didn't know my dark secret. How could she? She just saw the vicious side of me, without seeing what I had to pay in return. "Later, my dear Rain. Come, we have to go."

We slowed as we passed behind the dog as he took one step at a time toward the demon, forcing him back out of our way.

"Thank you, dog."

He gave a quick bark without taking his eyes off the creature. "Do me a favor. Save my pup. He's hiding from the demons out there. Take him to Salvation."

The desire to kill the demon was still strong, but feeling Rain at my leg reminded me of what my priorities were. "I will."

Once we left the cave it wasn't that difficult to find the dog's pup. His fear was an odor that led us right to the bush he hid under, shivering.

"It's okay," Rain said, going in after the pup. "My mom is Kills Like River, she can defeat anything, you'll be safe, I promise."

My heart hurt with love as I heard her talking to the pup, convincing him to come out of his hiding spot. This was my Rain, gentle of heart and capable of anything. And I was proud of her.

"Come on, we have to go quickly."

They both came out and we ran, as fast as we could until our chests hurt with every breath, and then we still ran. I had to carry the pup part of the way, but was impressed at how well Rain kept pace.

We ran up the side of a mountain, tiring with every step, but behind me I saw the demon lord chasing us. The dog had not been able to keep his Eye on him long enough.

The sky grew dark as we ran, which would only give the demons more power. They thrived in darkness. I didn't have time to search for the falling star. I knew it would rise soon, and would be even larger than the previous night. How many more nights until it fell?

Despite how much pain we were in neither of us stopped, until we reached the top and saw Salvation.

In the valley below lay the largest structure I had ever seen man make. It was almost like one of their houses, but entirely made of wood and taller than any of the trees around. Halfway up the ship was a large opening, with a ramp leading the way in. There was also a second, smaller opening nearby where the preacher stood, his arms held out as he cried to the humans below him.

The men shouted curses at the man as they waved torches in the air. Fire, a destructive force that only man had learned to harness. And they threatened to set Salvation on fire. Only a human could have the pride, arrogance, and sheer stupidity to turn their backs when salvation was offered.

A roar echoed off the rocky ledges. The demon lord was close.

"Get to Salvation," I cried out, pushing both of the young ones down the hill. They ran until their feet were almost tripping over themselves.

A few animals ran up the ramp that led to the belly of the beast still, some in pairs and some alone. Although the ones that were alone met up with their mate at the top of the ramp, where a young Velociraptor and small dog waited.

"You must get in here now," the priest shouted above the noise of the humans gathered at the base of the ramp. "The Lord has provided a way, you simply have to take it."

"We don't need you or your God," the men cried. One of them threw their torch onto the wooden structure and the others followed after.

I didn't know why the preacher tried so hard. They obviously didn't want to follow and most of these men were evil, wasn't the Creator trying to cleanse the land of evil? Why offer salvation to these?

"Quickly," I shouted. "Get up the ramp, I'll stop the demon from getting to Salvation."

The pup ran past the angry crowd and the fires that burned on the edge of the long structure, but Rain stopped and looked back.

I couldn't leave her without saying bye, no matter how close the demon was behind me. I ran to her and rubbed my muzzle against hers.

"You are my brave warrior," I said. I wanted to say more, but nothing seemed right. How did someone say good bye to their hatchling for the last time?

"I love you," was all I said as I pushed her toward the ramp. The humans blocked her path but I growled and they quickly backed away. None of them were willing to fight an angry Velociraptor, and then they saw the demon lord coming. Some of the humans liked the demons, trading their souls for more power and influence, but most understood that the demons would turn on their summoners as quickly as they would devour those souls sacrificed to summon them.

I couldn't do anything about the fires on Salvation, and I didn't think the humans would be much more of a threat, but the demon lord could break through the walls of Salvation and kill everything in there.

I charged up the hill toward the giant demon and the smaller ones he had gathered to his aid during his pursuit.

I Roared again from my soul. The demon lord stopped mid run as if he had hit a wall, while the smaller demons disintegrated into ashes and blew away with the wind. Those that were too far away to be affected by the Roar turned and fled in fear.

"I will destroy you," he shouted, with a voice that turned my stomach, "and I will destroy Salvation and every creature in there. Especially your hatchling. Then that abomination of a Roar that you have will never kill another spirit."

I could not allow this evil spirit to reach Salvation, no matter what it cost me.

The demon lord dodged my attack, but I caught his wing and clawed my way up to his back.

"You think you can stop me alone?" He shouted as he struggled to throw me off.

I Roared again, next to the demon lord's head, turning it gray and black. He fell to the ground, throwing me off in the process. The humans watched the fight, their obsession with the preacher and Salvation forgotten.

My head hurt, and my back stung from all the cuts I had received from the evil spirits earlier. I didn't want to keep fighting, I just wanted to sleep, but the thought of my Rain safe in Salvation pushed me to fight. I wasn't sure I could Roar again with how tired I was, but I had to try.

I saw her at the edge of the doorway, watching me with the other Velociraptor. I wouldn't let her see me give up.

The ground shook as the demon lord stood behind me and I forced myself up to face him. There was no way I could win this battle. I took a few slow steps, trying to fight through the dizziness that wanted to throw me to the ground.

The demon lord reached me, his hand coming down on me. I didn't have the energy to dodge the massive claw, so I didn't try. This would be it.

I closed my eyes and thought of Rain. The joy that I felt as I saw her break through her egg. The pride that I felt as she went on her first hunt, not letting how small she was compared to this new pack hold her back at all. I smiled as I remembered when she brought her first field mouse home, not eating it right away like the others would do, but bringing it held high to show me.

And then I smiled, as I thought about the future where Rain would have those same memories of her own hatchling, as they walked off Salvation and into a cleansed land where there was no sin and no demons. Every Velociraptor after this would be a hatchling of Saved From The Rain.

I took a deep breath and Roared, giving every bit of myself that I could into it. The demon's hand shattered as it reached me, throwing him to the ground.

I was exhausted, and barely stayed standing. I had stopped his attack, and destroyed his arm, but he would still destroy me.

Screams rose from the humans behind me and I risked a glance in their direction.

The massive door to Salvation swung closed on its own, blocking my view of Rain. The preacher, standing on a ledge fell to his knees and cried out in agony. "You fools! Salvation was offered to you freely and you refused. What comes next is on your own heads."

Then the preacher went inside Salvation and closed the small door at the top.

Everything was silent, even the wind. Nobody said anything as the humans stared at each other. They had shouted insults at the preacher while he stood on the ledge, and now it had seemed that they had won as the preacher retreated.

A loud rumble, louder than anything I had ever heard in my life knocked me to the ground as the star that had been growing larger finally fell from the sky.

It flew overhead with fire trailing behind it and disappeared over the mountains. My ears rang as I tried to recover and stand. The demon lord still seemed full of hatred, but the fight had gone out of him. We stood there for several minutes, and then water fell from the sky. The ground shook like an angry beast and broke apart as water shot out, spraying high into the sky and then falling back to the earth.

Rivers formed, washing out trees and rocks and crushing the humans that now pounded on the side of Salvation, begging to be let in, but the large door remained closed as the water rose and the ramp fell away. I panicked as a lake formed and threatened to cover Salvation if the rain didn't stop soon.

I scrambled, looking for some way to help, maybe dig a tunnel to lead the waters away? But there was too much. I cried out to the Creator. I didn't know if he would listen since I wasn't a shaman, but I cried out anyway as the rain continued to pour on my head. The water rose higher up the hill until it reached my legs.

Salvation groaned, and started to move! I watched as it rose off the ground, floating on top of the rising water like some kind of monstrous duck. As it rose I knew that my hatchling, and all the others in Salvation, would be safe as the rest of the world ended.

So this is rain, I thought. So gentle a thing, yet capable of destroying everything in its path to fulfill its purpose.

I hadn't known what rain was when I gave that name to my hatchling, but now I knew it was perfect.

THE END

J.L. Zenor is a Christian Fantasy and Science Fiction author. He currently has several short stories published, including Rite of Passage and Guardian, and several more appearing in anthologies such as Domesticated Velociraptors and Adventures in Zookeeping. While honing his skills of storytelling with short stories he is also working on planning an epic novel.

Jon lives in a castle in the mountains of Colorado with his family, where the deer regularly try to give him writing advice. (He usually ignores it…)

Check out all of Jon's stories on his website, http://JLZenor.com, and follow @JLZenor on Instagram, Twitter, or FaceBook.

TRUE ACCOUNTS FROM A FEW OF OUR AUTHORS

The Weight of Feathers
A True Memory
by
Sam Knight

Sometime last century, when I was young enough, but not too young, and old enough, but still not really old enough, I was given access to a BB gun. It was a pump-style; the wooden grip on the bottom of the barrel, where you rest your hand when you hold it to shoot, was actually a lever that you had to jack to build up enough air pressure to shoot the BB. If I remember right, it took about three pumps just to get enough air to make the BB come out of the barrel faster than gravity could have pulled it out. The maximum number of pumps was fifty.

I'm sure I tried more than that to see if it made any difference, but I don't really remember. I do remember pinching my fingers as the grip clicked flush with the barrel at the end of a pump. Nasty little blood blisters those were.

My point is, it took a good minute to ready the gun for a second shot, and by the time I was ready, my arms would be tired and shaky—not so good for aiming. I was a good shot and quickly tired of shooting a can on the side of the hill. (Tired in more ways than one!) I soon went after a couple of horseflies, a butterfly, anything that moved really, but even a shooter with my prowess had problems taking out an insect in flight. When the tiny yellow tweety bird presented itself high in the branches of a tree, I found myself unable to resist the temptation.

There was a puff of little yellow feathers that slowly drifted down, dissipating into the tree branches like a morning fog. I remember it vividly. I don't expect I could ever forget it if I wanted to.

I had taken a life.

There was no more happy little tweety bird, flitting from branch to branch, making tiny inquisitive peeping noises as it searched for insects to eat. There was only me, silence, and the memory of what had been there moments before.

That silence haunted me from the moment it began.

I found the tiny bird at the base of the tree. It was warm. It's tiny body so soft and supple in my hands, it was like a liquid somehow maintaining the semblance of a solid form, trying to flow between my fingers. There was neither a speck of blood nor sign of a wound, but the gaping hole in my soul was neither comforted nor mollified. In fact, it made it worse.

After a time, I felt I needed to bury it. Out of respect, out of sorrow, out of guilt. I couldn't stand the thought of dirt on its nearly perfect tiny body. (Only nearly perfect because it was now missing the most important part—the spark of life.) I also couldn't stand the thought of a coyote, or some other predator, digging it up.

As I walked along in a depressed stupor, I came across a stump, the remnants of a tree cut down by loggers nearly a century before, surrounded by brush tall or taller than I was. A miniature forest vale of sorts that, in my mind, felt like a holy place. The stump had a smooth flat, level surface from the work of the saw blade and it stood nearly waist high, unusual for the mid-shin height of most of the stumps, which where nearly all cut at proper felling angles.

I lay the bird on the stump and solemnly gathered stones, placing them on top of the little body, building a cairn. I made a large enough pile that in my young mind no coyote would be able to get under it. Not true, I know now, but still. I left it neatly stacked and formed into a decent sized, protective grave.

I came back to it that fall, maybe three months later, maybe less.

The little vale felt dull and lifeless, even amidst the red and yellow leaves of the brush lining it. The cairn still stood on the gray weathered stump, untouched by coyote or anything else. I had built it well.

But I was young, too young, really. And not nearly old enough. I hadn't made it proof against myself. Morbid curiosity overtook me, and I began removing stones, one by one, to see what lie beneath.

Of all the things I expected to see, I found the one thing I never would have guessed in a million years. Nothing. Not a skull, not a claw, not a single feather.

How is it possible to remove a skeleton from within a cairn without disturbing the cairn? A person could rebuild the cairn, I suppose. But no one knew about it except me, and it was hidden on private land. If someone had found it, why rebuild it?

Insects perhaps? Could they break down bone enough to remove through the tiny cracks? Could they, would they, remove all of the feathers from under the weight of all the rocks?

I don't know.

I do know I've never lost the regret and respect for life I gained on the day I encountered a tiny yellow bird, and I've never lost the wonder and hope I found the day I didn't encounter a tiny yellow bird.

J. D. Harrison

My very first encounter with an otherworldly animal came on a dark night of my adolescence, as I fled the pressures of sharing my summer camp experience with a clique of pre-teen girls who made it very clear I was not welcome among them. Though I remain grateful to the Girl Scouts for the chance to go to camp, for my one and only chance to be with the horses I felt so drawn to, the girls themselves weren't always so wonderful.

I picked my way up the hill behind our cabin, relying on the moon to guide me since I didn't want to risk using a flashlight, afraid to get in trouble for being out after curfew. Everything about that night clings to my memories, from the slip and crunch of old pine needles beneath my unlaced hiking boots, to the almost vanilla fragrance of the pines themselves, the warmth of the day having made something sweet out of their usual tar. I lost my footing at one point, reaching out to stop myself from falling, and my palm found purchase on a small granite boulder. To this day, I can look down at my hand and clearly recall the shape of the scab it made, the way it stung for days as I forced it to flex and sweat, unwilling to reveal it to my councilors. Not just for fear they would discover my indiscretion, but because it became a secret badge of what transpired that night, one that meant far more to me than any of the ones I'd stitched onto my bright green sash.

Once my heart rate recovered from the near accident, I pushed onward, determined to reach the top. While I couldn't go far, knowing a barbed wire fence limited the distance of my forbidden adventure, my goal was to get as close as I could to the horses. They were still more than a quarter of a mile away from our cabin unit, but just the thought of their nearness brought a peaceful sort of longing. I needed the acceptance they promised, so unlike my unforgiving peers. Horses took me as I was, not as they thought I should be. My wide hips, lack of breasts, and pimpled face meant nothing to them. All they cared about was how I made them feel.

Scrabbling the last few steps on my hands and knees, I finally reached the top. The air felt cleaner, so far away from the expectations placed on young girls, so much closer to what truly mattered to me. Muffling my harsh breathing in the collar of my jacket, I felt light headed with effort and accomplishment. I could barely make out the Ponderosa that surrounded me, so tall and straight as they stood sentinel. Their canopy hid most of the moon light, keeping my secret from the world.

A shiver of movement off to my right had me spinning in place, fearing I'd disturbed one of the bears that the counselors claimed populated the area. Even if I'd wanted to, I wouldn't have run. At that point in my life, I felt so powerless, and I would have yielded to an attack, somehow convinced I deserved it as punishment. But my now wide pupils detected no other shadows, no movement to speak of. Perhaps my guilt was getting the better of me?

I'd begun to relax when the noise came again, this time, the sound ringing familiar now that my panic had faded. After all, I'd heard it earlier that day, as we rode our horses along the trail, the crunching chuff of a hoof on the thick bed of the forest floor. Had one of the horses escaped their pasture? But as I stepped toward the noise, the moon broke through the trees, showing the little clearing held no one but me.

Two steps closer, the hooves moved, and though my mouth went dry with visceral terror, something deeper inside grew calm. Horses were safe. Though they might hurt me in fear for their lives, they would never attack me to make themselves feel better. They wouldn't seek my pain for their own ends, or pummel me with razor sharp words until I bled tears.

So, I drew on that bone deep faith, releasing the breath I held. In response, the hoof beats moved closer, bringing with it a presence I could feel. Each step increased the awareness, pressure building on my skin from the direction of its approach. Trembling with a combination of anticipation and left over adrenaline, I held out the back of my hand, inviting the visitor to take my scent.

Warm, damp air pressed out over the skin on my wrist, a gentle huff of breath I've now experienced a million times or more in my life with horses. Each time I feel it now, it still holds the same wonder that moment did, as if I'd been baptized, blessed, anointed. Though some may call it sacrilegious, it was one of the most spiritual, religious experiences of my life.

Would that the spirit had lingered, that I could tell a longer tale, but as I grew comfortable with my visitor, I reached out to touch. My fingers found nothing but a chill swath of air, but in less than a second, even that was gone. I waited for a long time, hoping it would return, but eventually, I returned to my cabin. The girls inside were all asleep, allowing me the peace to cherish the memory before their ugly words could sully it.

Now, I have nothing but this memory, one freshened by the magic I feel each time I greet a horse. Now, I know it lives on in those who read the accounting, keeping a spirit alive that seemed to recognize how much a young girl needed its benediction. Horses, alive or not, have the ability to touch the spirit in a way little else can.

Reese

By Rebecca McFarland Kyle

I believe in ghosts. Throughout my life, I've experienced transient presences both benign and not which re-enforce my belief.

Up until I moved into this house, the spirits I encountered remained to resolve some issue or aid in some way. For example, both my husband and I saw our dog Drew in the backyard of our former home after he'd been euthanized. Then, a friend adopted a similar breed dog Sarge who spent a couple of hours in the yard the weekend we sold that home and moved to Oregon.

Sarge always greeted me like a long-lost friend no matter how long we'd been apart. His tail would flag up over his back like a husky's. He'd lean up against me and sit on my right foot which is what Drew used to do. He never did that with any member of his new family. We theorize Drew remained with us to protect the house and the yard and then left to become part of another family when he knew we were going.

Occasionally, I would get a hint of something malevolent but nothing long-lasting. I walked into an open house once and walked right straight out.

Neither the realtor nor my husband could convince me to go back in.

I tried to convince my husband to stay out, but he wasn't listening. He instead climbed up in the attic and discovered the support beams were charred black. They were so porous from burning he could stick his pen several inches into them. He went back downstairs and asked the realtor about a fire and the man admitted that the house had burned and a family pet died in the blaze. They'd rebuilt the interior of the home, but apparently neglected the attic. Oddly, no one purchased that house and it was eventually torn down and replaced with a business.

I got no hint of anything wrong when we looked at the house we are living in now. The night we moved in, I had my first nightmare. I was standing outside in the cold and darkness as the house burned down with my husband and four cats trapped inside.

I woke up screaming.

For months after, I had nightmares every night. This was not a common occurrence. I often dreamed, but nightmares were infrequent and generally related to specific issues I could pin down and deal with either medically or emotionally.

The dreams were so bad I considered contacting a therapist when I awakened one night from a terrible dream of death and mayhem and realized something was in front of me. I hit the bedroom lights and saw an amorphous greenish shape on the wall. Having had eye-related difficulties, I knew to look away and see if the shape followed. No, the other walls, ceiling were clear.

Next, I realized Reese, my half-grown Siamese kitten, was huddled right beside me. He stared at the same spot on the wall where I saw the shape. A low angry growl emitted from his throat and a spiky ridge of tan fur stood up along his spine.

I first went cold with fear and then got angry. Something told me what we both were seeing was the source of my nightmares. I laid my hand on Reese's shoulders, felt the warmth of his fur and the strength of his presence.

"Get out of my house," I said to the presence. "If you don't leave now, my cat and I are going to send you straight to hell."

My ears popped. Reese stopped growling. Instead, I felt a resounding purr against my palm. I took several deep breaths and the two of us went back to sleep. We haven't been troubled by whoever that was since.

And yes, Reese still protects me. If my husband is around, he'll hide from repairmen, but if it's just me, he will stand between the stranger and me. He watches outside for any interloper on his property and gives us good warnings. He's a brave soul and a credit to his ancestors who were tasked to protect the ancient temples.

Death Greeting

By Dana Bell

Little One died in the wee hours of the morning. Her tiny, limp body lying on the dark fabric at the emergency vet's is an image burned into my mind. Her kidney's had failed and she'd been steadily declining for a couple of weeks. Allowing her release was my final mercy to her.

Monday at work I took a walk around the grounds. I normally did that anyway. Not even sure why I even bothered to go in. Better than staying home I guess.

I did feel guilty about her last hours being confined. My intent had been to protect her from the other cats who knew something was wrong. She'd always been the princess, the queen bee of the roost, respected by the other three.

My desire had been to hold her, but she'd been so far gone the vet insisted on putting Little One on an exam table. It hadn't felt right to me, even though I stroked her head and told her it was okay to go. I knew when she'd gone.

Two days later, standing in the bright sunshine, my heart broken, my companion girl gone, I cried.

Suddenly she was there. In her new body. Didn't quite look like her, but I knew it was Little One. She stepped out of from where she'd gone, rubbed against my ankle, I could feel her soft fur, and said her final goodbye. All had been forgiven.

A year and half later, when Tabitha took a turn for the worse and it was her turn to go, Little One appeared and the two were reunited. I still remember Little One playing with her long-time companion.

Years later, when Sammy went, the girls, and Dids, a cat I'd had many years ago, all appeared to take him with them. Dids even crawled along the back of the couch, nuzzling my neck, like he'd done so many times during his life when he'd draped himself on my shoulders.

I saw Sammy's spirit sitting between the girls, Tabitha grooming him.

They all came to get Max as well.

I've seen them all in special garden in heaven, one you enter by going between two golden inscribed pillars, playing together. Waiting for the day when I join them.

It will be a joyous reunion.

J. A. Campbell

Tiffany died while I was away at college. Mom called me and told me they had no choice but to put her to sleep, and while I was sad, she wasn't alone, and didn't have to suffer long at the end. I cried, and I missed her, but it wasn't the wrong decision, though another month and a half would have seen me home for the winter holiday and a chance to say goodbye. When I came home for the winter break, my family, still fresh with the English Setter's loss, said they still caught sight of her feathered tail flashing around a corner, or swore they heard her bark for the door whenever the bell rang. I didn't sense her at all on my first trip home, but I didn't disbelieve them.
Next time I came home I too caught sight of a white feathered tail now and again, and wouldn't have been surprised to hear a bark at the door, but it wasn't until my third time home that Tiffy came to say goodbye. It was near the end of my visit, and I was in that half awake, half asleep state when I felt her lay down next to my leg, as she often did when alive. I reached down to scratch her, and we lay there for a while.

When I finally woke, she was gone, and I never sensed her, nor caught a glimpse of her tail again. She said goodbye to all of us, and was able to finally move on. I'm glad she and I got to finally say goodbye.

If you enjoyed this collection, be sure to check out the other works in the Ghost Hunting Dog universe.

Brown Ghost Hunting Dog, Collection One

Have a ghost problem? Brown is the dog for the job. Normally used to herd sheep, her Border Collie Eye works on ghosts, too. Follow her adventures as she and her human, Elliott, hunt ghosts all over the old west. They find their first real ghost in a saloon in Miller, Colorado, and from there her nose leads her to more adventures.

Brown fights ghosts on trains, boats, and in old mines. She discovers that some ghosts are friendly when she and Elliott need extra help fighting a magical construct. There may be friendly ghosts, but there are no friendly Martians, and Brown has to take the ultimate adventure to save Elliott from their nefarious clutches, meeting new friends along the way.

Packed full of adventure, this weird western anthology contains seven short stories and one never before published novella.

Join Brown and her friends for more adventures in this second collection of ghost hunting fun. When she's not busy herding sheep, she uses her border collie eye to keep wayward spirits in line, whether it's banishing ghosts or solving murders. From abandoned forts, to haunted hotels, with Brown's nose for trouble she's always the dog for the job. This collection has nine action filled short stories perfect for anyone who loves dogs or a ghostly tale.